MUSIC: ITS LANGUAGE, HISTORY, AND CULTURE

A Reader for Core Curriculum 1.3

Revised Second Edition

RAY ALLEN

DOUGLAS COHEN

NANCY HAGER

JEFFREY TAYLOR

KENDALL/HUNT PUBLISHING COMPANY
4050 Westmark Drive   Dubuque, Iowa 52002

Cover art and design by Lisa Panazzolo
Photos by John Ricasoli

CONTENTS

INTRODUCTION

Welcome to Core Curriculum 1.3, *Music: Its Language History, and Culture.* The course has a number of interrelated objectives:

1. To introduce you to works representative of a variety of music traditions. These include the repertoires of Western Europe from the Middle Ages through the present; of the United States, including art music, jazz, folk, rock, musical theater; and from at least two non-Western world areas (Africa, Asia, Latin America, the Caribbean, the Middle East, Indian subcontinent).

2. To enable you to speak and write about the features of the music you study, employing vocabulary and concepts of melody, rhythm, harmony, texture, timbre, and form used by musicians.

3. To explore with you the historic, social, and cultural contexts and the role of class, ethnicity, and gender in the creation and performance of music, including practices of improvisation and the implications of oral and notated transmission.

4. To acquaint you with the sources of musical sounds—instruments and voices from different cultures, found sounds, electronically generated sounds; basic principles that determine pitch and timbre.

5. To examine the influence of technology, mass media, globalization, and transnational currents on the music of today.

The chapters in this reader contain definitions and explanations of musical terms and concepts, short essays on subjects related to music as a creative performing art, biographical sketches of major figures in music, and historical and cultural background information on music from different periods and places. The reader also contains a membership card to Rhapsody, an online music source, that will give you access for the semester to the musical works assigned by your instructor as well as to thousands of other recorded items available through that site.

CHAPTER 1: ELEMENTS OF SOUND AND MUSIC

Making music has been an activity of human beings, both as individuals and with others, for thousands of years. Written texts, pictorial representations, and folklore sources provide evidence that people from all over the globe and from the beginnings of recorded history have created and performed music for religious rituals, civil ceremonies, social functions, story telling, and self-expression. Some of the terminology, concepts, and vocabulary used by musicians in writing and talking about the many types of music you will be studying are discussed in this section on elements of sound and music.

Elements of Sound

From the perspective of a musician, anything that is capable of producing sound is a potential instrument for musical exploitation. What we perceive as sound are vibrations (sound waves) traveling through a medium (usually air) that are captured by the ear and converted into electrochemical signals that are sent to the brain to be processed.

Since sound is a wave, it has all of the properties attributed to any wave, and these attributes are the four elements that define any and all sounds. They are the frequency, amplitude, wave form and duration, or in musical terms, pitch, dynamic, timbre (tone color), and duration.

Element	Musical Term	Definition
Frequency	Pitch	How high or low
Amplitude	Dynamic	How loud or soft
Wave form	Timbre	Unique tone color of each instrument
Duration	Duration	How long or short

Frequency
The frequency, or pitch, is the element of sound that we are best able to hear. We are mesmerized when a singer reaches a particularly high note at the climax of a song, just as we are when a dancer makes a spectacularly difficult leap. We feel very low notes (low pitches) in a physical way as well, sometimes expressing dark or somber sentiments as in music by country singers like Johnny Cash, and other times as the rhythmic propulsion of low-frequency pulsations in electronically amplified dance music.

The ability to distinguish pitch varies from person to person, just as different people are better and less capable at distinguishing different colors (light frequency). Those who are especially gifted recognizing specific pitches are said to have "perfect pitch." On the other hand, just as there are those who have difficulty seeing the difference in colors that are near each other in the light spectrum (color-blind), there are people who have trouble identifying pitches that are close to each other. If you consider yourself to be such a "tone-deaf" person, do not fret. The great American composer Charles Ives considered the singing of the tone-deaf caretaker at his church to be some of the most genuine and expressive music he experienced.

An audio compact disc is able to record sound waves that vibrate as slow as 20 times per second (20 Hertz = 20 Hz) and as fast as 20,000 times per second (20,000 Hertz = 20 kiloHertz = 20 kHz). Humans are able to perceive sounds from approximately 20 Hz to 15 kHz, depending on age, gender, and noise in the environment. Many animals are able to perceive sounds much higher in pitch.

When musicians talk about being "in tune" and "out of tune," they are talking about pitch, but more specifically, about the relationship of one pitch to another. In music we often have a succession of pitches, which we call a melody, and also play two or more pitches at the same time, which we call harmony. In both cases, we are conscious of the mathematical distance between the pitches as they follow each other horizontally (melody) and vertically (harmony). The simpler the mathematical relationship between the two pitches, the more consonant it sounds and the easier it is to hear if the notes are in tune.

The simplest relationship of one pitch to another is called the octave. The octave is so fundamental that we give two pitches an octave apart the same letter name. The ratio between notes an octave apart is 2:1. If we have a note vibrating at 400 Hz, the pitch an octave higher vibrates at 800 Hz (2 * 400 Hz). The pitch an octave lower than 400 Hz has a frequency of 200 Hz (400 Hz / 2).

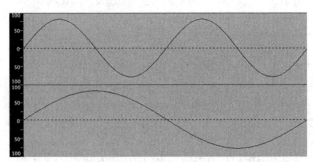
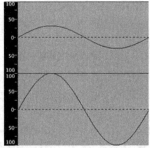

Example 1.1 Two sound waves one octave apart. The bottom is 1/400th of a second of a sine wave vibrating at 400 Hz.

Example 1.2 Two sound waves with the same frequency, the top is 10 db softer than the bottom.

Amplitude
Amplitude is the amount of energy contained in the sound wave and is perceived as being either loud or soft. Amplitude is measured in decibels, but our perception of loud and soft changes depending on the sounds around us. Walking down a busy street at noon where the noise in the environment might average 50 decibels, we would find it difficult to hear the voice of a person next to us speaking at 40 decibels. On that same street at night that 40 decibel speaking voice will seem like a shout when the surrounding noise is only about 30 decibels.

Wave Form
The wave form of a sound determines the tone color, or timbre that we hear and is how we can tell the difference between the sound produced by a voice, a guitar, and a saxophone even if they are playing the same frequency at the same amplitude.

The simplest wave form is the sine wave, which we have seen diagrammed in the examples for frequency and amplitude above. Pure sine waves rarely occur in nature but they can easily be created through electronic means. An instrument with a timbre close to the purity of a sine wave is the flute. The violin section of the orchestra, by contrast, has a much more complex timbre as seen in its wave form below.

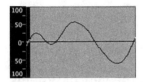

Example 1.3 Wave form of a solo flute.

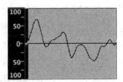

Example 1.4 Wave form of a violin string section.

Duration
Every sound event has its unique duration, which we perceive as being either short or long, depending on the context. Several durations, one after another, create the rhythm of a piece.

Elements of Music

Rhythm
All music involves the unfolding of sounds in time. Some of the terminology used in describing music therefore refers to the durational and temporal organization of musical sounds. The attack points of a sequence of sounds produce **rhythm**. The three syllables of the word "strawberry" can be pronounced at evenly spaced intervals (straw-ber-ry), or the first syllable can be stretched out, producing one long and two shorter durations (straaaaw-ber-ry)—two different speech rhythms. The speech rhythm of "My country, 'tis of thee" moves in evenly spaced syllables up to "tis," which is elongated, followed by "of," which is cut short and leads directly to "thee"—ta ta ta taaa t-ta. In both vocal and instrumental music, rhythm is generated by the onset of new sounds, whether the progression from one word or syllable to the next in a song, the succession of pitches of a violin melody, the striking of a drum, or the strumming of chords on a guitar.

Meter
The succession of attacks and durations that produces rhythm may proceed in a quite unpredictable flow ("to be or not to be, that is the question"—the opening of Hamlet's soliloquy)—what is called **nonmetered** or **free rhythm**—or may occur so as to create an underlying **pulse** or **beat** ("bubble, bubble, toil and trouble"—four beats coinciding with buh–buh–toil–truh—from the witches' incantation in Macbeth). Recurrent groupings of beats by two's, three's, or some combination of two's and three's, produces **meter.** The first beat of each metric group is often described as accented to characterize its defining function in the rhythmic flow (My country 'tis of thee, sweet land of liberty, of thee I sing—six groups of three beats, each beginning with the underlined syllable).

Another important rhythmic phenomenon is **syncopation**, which signifies irregular or unexpected stresses in the rhythmic flow (for example, straw-ber-ry instead of straw-ber-ry). A distinctive sequence of longs and shorts that recurs throughout an individual work or groups of works, such as particular dance types, is called a **rhythmic pattern, rhythmic figure,** or **rhythmic motive**.

Pitch
Pitch refers to the location of a musical sound in terms of low or high. As we have seen, in terms of the physics of sound, pitch is determined by frequency, or the number of vibrations per second: the faster a sounding object vibrates, the higher its pitch.

Although the audible range of frequencies for human beings is from about 20 to under 20,000 vibrations per second, the upper range of musical pitches is only around 4,000 vibrations per second. Frequency is determined by the length and thickness of the vibrating object. In general, longer and thicker objects vibrate more slowly and produce lower pitches than shorter and thinner ones. Thus, men's voices are usually lower than those of women and children, who have comparatively shorter and thinner vocal cords. The same principle is visible in the construction of many instruments. The longest wooden bars of a xylophone produce the lowest pitches, the shortest produce the highest. The alto saxophone is smaller and has a higher range than the slightly larger tenor saxophone.

Pitch, like temperature, is a sliding scale of infinite gradations. All theoretical systems of music organize this pitch continuum into successions of discrete steps analogous to the degrees on a thermometer. And just as the Fahrenheit and Celsius systems use different sized increments to measure temperature, different musical cultures have evolved distinctive pitch systems. The conventional approach to classifying pitch material is to construct a **scale**, an arrangement of the pitch material of a piece of music in order from low to high (and sometimes from high to low as well). Each element of a scale is called a "step" and the distance between steps is called an **interval**. Most Western European music is based on **diatonic** scales—seven-tone scales comprised of five "whole steps" (moderate-size intervals) and two "half steps" (small intervals). The position of the whole and half steps in the ascending ladder of tones determines the **mode** of the scale. Major and minor are two commonly encountered modes, but others are used in folk music, in Western European music before 1700, and in jazz. Another important scale type particularly associated with music from China, Japan, Korea, and other Asian cultures is **pentatonic**, a five-note scale comprised of three whole steps and two intervals of a step and a half.

The starting pitch of a scale is called the **tonic** or keynote. Most melodies end on the tonic of their scale, which functions as a point of rest, the pitch to which the others ultimately gravitate in the unfolding of a melody. **Key** is the combination of tonic and scale type. Beethoven's Fifth Symphony is in C minor because its basic musical materials are drawn from the minor scale that starts on the pitch C.

Melody

A succession of musical tones perceived as constituting a meaningful whole is called a **melody**. By its very nature, melody cannot be separated from rhythm. A musical tone has two fundamental qualities, pitch and duration, and both of these enter into the succession of pitch plus duration that constitutes a melody.

Melody can be synonymous with tune, but the melodic dimension of music also encompasses configurations of tones that may not be singable or particularly tuneful. Conversely, music may employ pitch material but not have a melody, as is the case with some percussion music. Attributes of melody include its compass, that is, whether it spans a wide or narrow range of pitches, and whether its movement is predominantly **conjunct** (moving by step and therefore smooth in contour) or **disjunct** (leaping to non-adjunct tones and therefore jagged in contour). Melodies may occur without additional parts (monophony), in combination with other melodies (polyphony), or supported by harmonies (homophony)—see the following discussion about Texture.

Melodies may be designed like sentences, falling into clauses, or **phrases**. Indeed, in composing vocal music, composers generally design melodies to parallel the structure and syntax of the text they are setting. The termination of a musical phrase is called a **cadence**. A full cadence functions like a period, punctuating the end of a complete musical thought. A half cadence is analogous to a comma, marking a pause or intermediate point of rest within a phrase. The refrain of *Jingle Bells*, for example, contains four phrases with three half cadences and a concluding full cadence:

Jingle bells, jingle bells, jingle all the way (half cadence)
Oh, what fun it is to ride in a one horse open sleigh (half cadence)
Jingle bells, jingle bells, jingle all the way (half cadence)
Oh, what fun it is to ride in a one horse open sleigh (full cadence, melody descends to the tonic)

In another melodic style, associated more with instrumental than vocal music, melodic material is not organized in regular, balanced units, but spins out in a long, continuous line.

Texture

Like fabric, music has a **texture,** which may be dense or transparent, thick or thin, heavy or light. Musical texture also refers to how many different layers of sound are heard at once, to whether these layers have a primarily melodic or an accompaniment function, and to how the layers relate to each other. A texture of a single, unaccompanied melodic line is called **monophony** from the Greek "*monos*" (single, alone) and "*phone*" (sound). Monophony becomes **heterophony** when spontaneous variations of two or more performers produce different versions of the same melody at the same time. The simultaneous combination of two or more independent melodies is classified as **polyphony** and of two or more simultaneous rhythmic lines as **polyrhythm.** Another principal textural category is **homophony**, one dominant melody with accompaniment. These classifications are often useful in describing individual works and repertory groups, but in practice many works and styles do not fall neatly into one category. For example, a common texture in jazz entails some instruments whose interaction would be described as polyphonic and others whose function it is to accompany them.

Two important concepts in the analysis and description of musical textures are counterpoint and harmony. **Counterpoint** refers to the conduct of simultaneously sounding melodic lines, one against the other. Rhythmic counterpoint denotes the unfolding of concurrent rhythmic parts in polyrhythmic textures. While counterpoint focuses on linear events, **harmony** is concerned with the vertical combination of tones that produces chords and successions of chords.

The Western system of musical notation, while somewhat limited in the expression of subtleties of rhythm and pitch, can indicate many simultaneous sounds and has enabled Western composers to create music of greater textural complexity than that of any other musical tradition. Principles or rules of composing multipart, or contrapuntal, music were first formulated during the Middle Ages and have evolved and changed to reflect new musical aesthetics, performance practices, and compositional techniques.

Tone Color

Tone color, or timbre, is the distinctive quality of a voice or instrument. Tone color is the result of an acoustic phenomenon known as overtones. In addition to the fundamental frequency heard as a sound's pitch, musical tones contain patterns of higher frequencies. Though these higher frequencies, or overtones, are not usually perceived as pitches in themselves, their relative presence or absence determines the characteristic quality of a particular voice or instrument. The prominence of overtones in musical instruments depends on such factors as the materials from which they are made, their design, and how their sound is produced. Similarly, the individual physiology of each person's vocal cords produces a unique speaking and singing voice. The term tone color suggests an analogy with the visual arts, and indeed the exploration, manipulation, and combination of instrumental and vocal sound qualities by performers and composers may be compared to the use of color by painters. Terms such as **orchestration, scoring,** and **arranging** refer to the aspect of composition that involves the purposeful treatment of tone color. A composer may choose to use pure colors (for example, the melody played by violins) or mixed colors (the melody played by violins and flutes), or to exploit a particular quality of an instrument, such as the unique sound of the clarinet in its low range. The art of orchestration encompasses various performance techniques that affect tone color, among them the use of mutes, which are devices for altering the sound of an instrument. In violins and other bowed strings, the mute is a small comb-shaped device that is clamped on the strings, making the sound veiled and somewhat nasal. Brass instruments are muted by inserting various materials into the bell.

Although tone color has a scientific explanation, its function in music is aesthetic. Music is an art of sound, and the quality of that sound has much to do with our response to it. Indeed, the concept of tonal beauty varies considerably in different periods, styles, and cultures. On the other hand, within a particular context, ideals of beauty may be quite firmly established and performers often pay extraordinary prices for instruments that can produce that ideal sound. But no instrument automatically produces a beautiful tone, so the finest violin will produce a rasping, scraping sound in the hands of a beginner. Even at the most advanced stages of accomplishment, achieving what is considered to be a beautiful tone is a criterion of a good performance.

The attitude toward tone color has played an interesting role in the history of Western art music. Prior to the 18th century, composers were often quite vague, even indifferent, with respect to how their musical ideas would be realized. It was customary to play music on whatever instruments were at hand and to perform some or all parts of vocal compositions on instruments. During the 18th century, as composers became more sensitive to the idiomatic quality of instruments, they began to conceive musical ideas in terms of particular tone colors. In the 19th and 20th centuries, the fascination with expanding and experimenting with the palette of tone colors has elevated the art of orchestration to a level equal to other aspects of the compositional process.

Form

The interaction of such elements as melody, rhythm, texture, and harmony in the unfolding of a musical work produces *form*. Most music conforms to one of the following three basic formal prototypes:

1. sectional, falling into units of contrasting or repeating content,
2. continuous, usually involving the development and transformation of one or more germinal ideas,
3. a combination of sectional and continuous.

In addition, four general concepts help in the appreciation of many forms: repetition, contrast, return, and variation. The concept of "return" is especially important, for when listeners hear something familiar (that is, something they heard earlier in a work or performance) the sense of "going home" can be very powerful, whether it takes place in a 45-minute symphony or a four-minute pop song. One traditional method of representing these concepts is to use letters of the alphabet to identify individual phrases or sections, AA indicating repetition, AB contrast, ABCD a continuous structure, ABA return, and ABACA a design involving contrast, repetition and return. Capital and lower case letters may be used to distinguish between different levels of formal organization, while symbols for prime (A', B' etc) signify restatement of material with some changes. When a section is repeated more than once with different changes, additional prime symbols may be used (ABA'CA", for example, where the second and third A's are both versions of the original "A," but different from each other).

To illustrate, the chorus of *Jingle bells* would be represented as *abab'* (*a* for the repeated music of the first and third lines, *b* and *b'* for the contrasting music of the second and fourth phrases with their different endings -half and full cadences, respectively). The entire song is in ABA form (A for Jingle bells....open sleigh), B for the second section of the song (Dashing through the snow...) and A for the return of the chorus.

In variation form, a melody or chord progression is presented successively in different versions; the form could be diagrammed as A A' A" A'" and so forth. Changes may be made in key, instrumentation, rhythm, or any number of ways, but the original tune is always recognizable. Aaron Copland's variations on the Shaker tune *Simple Gifts* in his *Appalachian Spring* is a famous example of variation on a tune, while Pachelbel's *Canon in D* might be considered a series of variations on a chord progression. Some have compared a jazz performance to a kind of variation form, where musicians play a pre-existing tune and then provide a series of improvised "variations" on that tune.

CHAPTER 2: MUSICAL INSTRUMENTS AND ENSEMBLES

Instruments: A World View

Though one could say that the human voice was the first instrument, most cultures have developed other distinctive ways of creating musical sound, from something as simple as two sticks struck together to the most complex pipe organ or synthesizer. Learning about musical instruments can teach you much about a culture's history and aesthetics, and there are a few general questions that are useful to ask, especially if an instrument is unfamiliar.

- What material is it made of? The physical composition of an instrument will often reflect the area in which it was developed; for example, certain types of wood or ceramics could indicate a specific geographical region. In addition, the instrument may be made of materials considered sacred by its culture, or be decorated in such a way that reflects its significance to the people who play it.

- How is sound produced? As seen below, there are a variety of ways in which an instrument can create sound.

- How is the instrument viewed by the culture that created it? Although in some cultures instruments are simply viewed as objects used in a musical performance, in others instruments are viewed as sacred or as part of a distinctive cultural ritual.

- Performance technique. As varied as are the shapes, sizes, and materials of musical instruments throughout the world is the manner in which they are played, whether struck, blown, bowed, shaken, etc. Often one instrument can be played in a variety of ways: For example, a violin can be bowed, plucked, struck, or even strummed like a guitar.

- Tone color/timbre. Related to an instrument's physical makeup and performance technique is the quality of its sound: It may be harsh and rough, or smooth and rich. Often an instrument's timbre will bring to mind colors or sensations that are difficult to describe.

- Range. An instrument's range has to do with the distance between the lowest note and the highest note it can produce. As with the human voice, many instruments have a particular part of the range that is preferred for its pleasing qualities, and one part of an instrument's range may sound very different from another (for example, the low range of the clarinet has an entirely different timbre than the upper register).

- How is the instrument used? An instrument may be used alone, or gathered with other instruments in ensembles.

Ethnomusicologists have devised a series of categories to classify instruments throughout the world, based on the ways in which they produce sound. Each of these words ends with the suffix *"phone,"* the Greek word for sound. The following are just the most general categories; each can be divided into subcategories, but we won't be worrying about those in this class.

- **Aerophones:** sound produced by air. Aerophones use many mechanisms to make the air in the instrument vibrate, thus creating sound waves. If you have ever blown across the top of a soda bottle, you've created an aerophone. Blowing across the bottle's opening splits the air so some goes across the opening and some goes into the bottle, thus creating vibrations. If you fill the bottle partially with water, the sound is higher, because the column of air in the bottle is shorter. In a trumpet, the vibration of air is created by the buzzing of the lips into a mouthpiece. Many instruments also use reeds—small, thin pieces of wood or bamboo—that vibrate as the air passes them, thus creating another distinctive sound.

- **Chordophones:** sound produced by strings. Both a rubber band stretched over a shoe box and a violin could be considered chordophones, as sound is produced by the vibration of a chord (or string). As mentioned above, chordophones can be played in a variety of ways: They can be plucked, struck, strummed, or played with a device known as a bow.

- **Membranophones:** sound produced by a stretched membrane (plastic, animal skin, fiberglass, etc.). The most familiar membranophones are the nearly infinite varieties of drums found throughout the world.

- **Idiophones:** sound produced by the body of the instrument itself. The word "idiophone" comes from the Greek "*id*" or "self." When you clap your hands together, you are essentially using them as idiophones, as it is the hands themselves that create the sound. Two sticks knocked together could be considered an idiophone, as well as any number of types of bells, where the entire instrument is struck and vibrates. A gourd filled with beads or seeds (or a maraca) would also be considered an idiophone, because it is the interior material hitting the sides of the instrument that create the sound.

- **Electrophones:** sound produced by electric or electronic means. This is a relatively new category that includes instruments such as synthesizers, computers, etc.

Human Voice as Instrument

The human voice is a natural musical instrument and singing by people of all ages, alone or in groups, is an activity in all human cultures. The human voice is essentially a wind instrument, with the lungs supplying the air, the vocal cords setting up the vibrations, and the cavities of the upper throat, mouth, and nose forming a resonating chamber. Different pitches are obtained by varying the tension of the opening between the vocal cords.

In the Western tradition, voices are classified according to their place in the pitch spectrum, soprano, mezzo soprano, and alto being the respective designations for the high, middle, and low ranges of women's voices, and tenor, baritone, and bass for men's. A counter tenor or contra tenor is a male singer with the range of an alto. These terms are applied not only to voices and singers but also to the parts they sing.

The range of an individual's voice is determined by the physiology of the vocal cords. However, because the vocal cords are muscles, even the most modest singing activity can increase their flexibility and elasticity, and serious training can do so to a remarkable degree. Singers also work to extend the power of their voices, control pitch, and quality at all dynamic levels, and develop speed and agility.

Vocal quality and singing technique are other important criteria in the classification of voices. A singer's tone color is determined in part by anatomical features, which include the mouth, nose, and throat as well as the vocal cords. But the cultivation of a particular vocal timbre is also strongly influenced by aesthetic conventions and personal taste. A tight, nasal tone is associated with many Asian and Arabic traditions, whereas opera and gospel singers employ a chest voice with pronounced vibrato. Even within a single musical tradition there may be fine distinctions based on the character and color of the voice. For example, among operatic voices, a lyric soprano has a light, refined quality and a dramatic soprano a powerful, emotional tone.

Most music for the voice involves the delivery of words. Indeed, speech itself, which is characterized by both up and down pitch inflections and durational variations of individual sounds, could be considered a primitive form of melody. The pitches of normal speech are relatively narrow in range, neither a robot-like monotone nor extremes of high and low, but even these modest fluctuations are important in punctuating the flow of ideas and communicating emotion. The setting of words to music involves the purposeful shaping of melodic and other musical elements and can invest a text with remarkable expressive power.

Vocal music is often identified as sacred or secular on the basis of its text. Sacred music may be based on a scriptural text, the words of a religious ceremony, or deal with a religious subject. The words in secular music may express feelings, narrate a story, describe activities associated with work or play, comment on social or political situations, convey a nationalistic message, and so on.

Western Categories of Instruments

Instruments are commonly classified in families, according to their method of generating sounds. The most familiar designations for these groupings are strings (sound produced by vibrating strings), winds (by a vibrating column of air), and percussion (by an object shaken or struck).

The members of the string family of the Western orchestra are violin, viola, cello (or violoncello), and bass (or double bass). All are similar in structure and appearance and also quite homogeneous in tone color, although of different pitch ranges because of differences in the length and diameter of their strings. Sound is produced by drawing a horsehair bow across the strings, less often by plucking with the fingertips (called pizzicato). The harp is also a member of the orchestral string family.

In wind instruments, the player blows through a mouthpiece that is attached to a conical or cylindrical tube filled with air. The winds are subdivided into woodwinds and brass. The nomenclature of the orchestral winds can be both confusing and misleading. For example, the modern flute, classified as a woodwind, is made of metal while ancestors of some modern brass instruments were made of wood; the French horn is a brass instrument, but the English horn is a woodwind; and the saxophone, a relatively new instrument associated principally with jazz and bands, is classified as a woodwind because its mouthpiece is similar to that of the clarinet, although its body is metal.

The main orchestral woodwinds are flute, clarinet, oboe, and bassoon. Their very distinctive tone colors are due in part to the different ways in which the air in the body of the instrument is set in vibration. In the flute (and the piccolo) the player blows into the mouthpiece at a sharp angle, in the clarinet into a mouthpiece with a single reed, and in the oboe and bassoon (also the less common English horn) through two reeds bound together. In all woodwinds, pitch is determined by varying the pressure of the breath in conjunction with opening and closing holes along the side of the instrument, either with the fingers or by keys and pads activated by the fingers.

The members of the brass family are wound lengths of metal tubing with a cup-shaped mouthpiece at one end and a flared bell at the other. Pitch is controlled in part by the pressure of the lips and amount of air, and also by altering the length of tubing either by valves (trumpet, French horn, tuba) or by a sliding section of tube (trombone).

The percussion family encompasses a large and diverse group of instruments, which in the Western system of classification are divided into pitched and nonpitched. The nucleus of the orchestral percussion section consists of two, three, or four timpani, or kettledrums. Timpani are tuned to specific pitches by varying the tension on the head that is stretched over the brass bowl. The snare drum, bass drum, triangle, cymbals, marimba (or xylophone), tambourine, castanets, and chimes are among the other instruments found in the percussion section of an orchestra when called for in particular musical works. Percussionists usually specialize in a particular instrument but are expected to be competent players of them all.

The piano, harpsichord, and organ constitute a separate category of instruments. The harpsichord might be classified as a plucked string, the piano as both a string and a percussion instrument since its strings are struck by felt-covered hammers, and the organ as a wind instrument, its pipes being a collection of air-filled tubes. Because the mechanism of the keyboard allows the player to produce several tones at once, keyboard instruments have traditionally been treated as self-sufficient rather than as members of an orchestral section.

Counterparts to the Western orchestral instruments are found in musical cultures all over the world. Among the strings are the Indian sitar, the Japanese koto, the Russian balalaika, and the Spanish guitar. Oboe-type instruments are found throughout the Middle East and bamboo flutes occur across Asia and Latin America. Brass-like instruments include the long straight trumpets used by Tibetan monks and instruments made from animal horns and tusks, such as the Jewish shofar. Percussion instruments are probably the most numerous and diverse, from simple folk instruments like gourd rattles filled with pebbles, notched sticks rubbed together, and hollow log drums, to the huge tempered metal gongs of China, the bronze xylophones of Indonesia, and the tuned steel drums of the Caribbean.

Ensembles

The word "ensemble" comes from the French meaning "together" and is a broad concept that encompasses groupings of various constituencies and sizes. Ensembles can be made up of singers alone, instruments alone, singers and instruments together, two performers or hundreds. Ensemble performance is part of virtually every musical tradition. Examples of large ensembles are the symphony orchestra, marching band, jazz band, West Indian steel pan orchestra, Indonesia gamelan, African drum ensembles, chorus, and gospel choir. In such large groups, performers are usually divided into sections, each with its particular material or function. So, for example, all the tenors in a chorus sing the same music, and all the alto saxes in a jazz big band play the same part. Usually a conductor or lead performer is responsible for keeping everyone together.

The large vocal ensemble most familiar to Westerners is the *chorus*, twenty or more singers grouped in soprano, alto, tenor, and bass sections. The designation *choir* is sometimes used for choruses that sing religious music. There is also literature for choruses comprised of men only, women only, and children. Small vocal ensembles, in which there are one to three singers per part, include the chamber chorus and barber shop quartet. Vocal ensemble music is sometimes intended to be performed a cappella, that is, by voices alone, and sometimes with instruments. Choral numbers are commonly included in operas, oratorios, and musicals.

The most important large instrumental ensemble in the Western tradition is the *symphony orchestra*. Orchestras such as the New York Philharmonic, Brooklyn Philharmonic, and those of the New York City Opera and Metropolitan Opera, consist of 40 or more players, depending on the requirements of the music they are playing. The players are grouped by family into sections – winds, brass, percussion and strings. Instruments from different sections frequently double each other, one instrument playing the same material as another, although perhaps in different octaves. Thus, while a symphony by Mozart may have parts for three sections, the melody given to the first violins is often identical to that of the flutes and clarinets; the bassoons, cellos and basses may join forces in playing the bass line supporting that melody while the second violins, violas, and French horns are responsible for the pitches that fill out the harmony. The term orchestration refers to the process of designating particular musical material to particular instruments.

The origins of the orchestra in Western Europe date back to the early baroque and the rise of opera, for which composers wrote instrumental overtures, accompaniments to vocal numbers, and dances. In this early period, the ensemble typically consisted of about 16 to 20 strings plus a harpsichord, called the continuo, that doubled the bass line and filled out the harmonies. Other instruments could be included, but primarily as soloists rather than regular members. The designation *chamber orchestra* is sometimes applied to these early orchestras, reflecting the fact that, during the Baroque period, orchestral music was often composed as entertainment for the nobility and performed in the rooms, or chambers, of their palaces, rather than the large concert halls of today.

During the classical period, the orchestra expanded in size to between 40 and 60 players. Strings remain the heart of the ensemble, but there are more of them, and by the early 19th century, pairs of flutes, oboes, clarinets, bassoons, French horns, trumpets and timpani had become standard members. For the most part, the woodwinds double the strings, the horns fill out the harmonies, and the trumpets and timpani add rhythmic emphasis. For many composers of the 19th century, exploring the timbral possibilities of the orchestra became an increasingly important aspect of the creative process. The ensemble of the romantic period grew to 80 or more players through the increase in the numbers of instruments of the classical orchestra and the addition of new ones – piccolo, English horn, contrabassoon, trombone, tuba, harp, celeste, cymbals, triangle, a variety of drums. Scores also called for special effects such as muting – muffling or altering the sound of string instruments by placing a wooden clamp placed across the bridge, or brass instruments by inserting material into the bell. There is no single concept of the orchestra in the 20th century. Composers have written for chamber ensembles and for gigantic forces; they have used traditional instrumentations but also further extended the palette of musical tone colors by incorporating non-western instruments, invented instruments, electronically altered instruments, and non-musical sound sources such as sirens. Some have approached the orchestra not as the deliverer of melody, rhythm, and harmony, but as a palette of tone colors, to be mixed, juxtaposed, manipulated, ordered, and experienced as a sonic collage.

The ***jazz big band*** is another example of a large ensemble. The instruments are typically divided into the reed section (saxes, sometimes clarinets), the brass section (trumpets, trombones, sometimes cornets), and the rhythm section (commonly piano, guitar, string bass, and drum set). The rhythm section – which appears in most groups, large and small – is responsible for maintaining the rhythm (hence the name) as well as the harmony on which the featured soloists are improvising. Because of their size, jazz big bands often play from written arrangements (see Chapter 7: Jazz)

The ***gamelan*** of Indonesia is an example of a large non-Western ensemble. The distinctive sound of the gamelan is created by metallophones, that is, instruments made of metal and struck with a mallet. Some resemble small, medium, and large xylophones, but with tuned bars of bronze instead of wood. Some look like a collection of lidded cooking kettles of different sizes. The layers of melody created by these instruments are punctuated by gongs, chimes, and drums. The gamelan accompanies ceremonial plays and dances and is deeply connected to religious rituals. The instruments themselves are charged with charismatic power and are often intricately carved and brilliantly painted with figures and designs that replicate elements of cosmological forces.

Another type of grouping found in many musical traditions consists of a small number of players – from 2 to 8 or 9 – each of whom has a separate, unique part. An important feature of small ensembles is an overall balance among the individual performers, so that one does not overpower the others. Instead, every member of the group plays an essential role in the presentation and development of musical ideas. Instead of a conductor, the performers rely on eye contact, careful listening and sensitivity to each other that may have developed over years of rehearsing and playing together. In the western classical tradition, such small groups are classified as ***chamber ensembles*** and include the string quartet (2 violins, viola, cello), piano trio (piano, violin, cello), and wind quintet (flute, oboe, clarinet, bassoon, French horn). A comparable small group in jazz is a ***jazz combo***. Like the jazz big band, the jazz combo uses a rhythm section, but in place of reed and brass sections, a handful of additional improvising instruments. One preferred combination is the jazz quintet, made up of trumpet, saxophone, and rhythm section of piano, bass, and drums. Miles Davis's famous quintet of the 1960s used this instrumentation. Other examples of small instrumental groupings include a bluegrass band, Klezmer band, rock band, and trio of players of Indian ragas.

CHAPTER 3: COMPOSER, PERFORMER, AUDIENCE

Composition and performance are related and sometimes inseparable activities in the creation of music (as they are also in theater and dance). In the Western tradition, the roles of performer and composer have often been the province of separate people, a composer, playwright, or choreographer authoring a work that is then brought to life by others who are skilled as instrumentalists/vocalists, actors, or dancers. Compositions are preserved in some kind of written form or passed on through oral tradition. The "work" thus has an existence that is separate from its performance; it is an independent entity to be brought to life each time it is performed, or re-created. Conservatory training in the performing arts typically covers both creative and interpretative functions, and individuals frequently cross over from one to the other.

In traditions heavily based on improvisation, such as Indian classical music, African tribal music, and jazz, the performers are the composers and the performance is the work. Improvisations are sometimes recorded, or later written down based on memory. But evanescence is a defining aspect of extemporaneous creation. Many performance traditions involve preexisting material that the performer is expected to flesh out in the course of performance. Indeed, some degree of spontaneity is part of any live performance and no two performances of the same work, no matter how meticulously notated, will be identical. Whatever the relationship between creation and performance, composition is a highly disciplined art that requires mastery over often very sophisticated materials and a creative impulse whose origins and mental processes remain a mystery.

Performance practice refers to the conventions and customs associated with the performance of a particular musical repertory—for example, the instruments employed, techniques of singing, and the nature and extent of improvisation that are expected.

Prior to the invention of recording technologies, how music actually sounded had to be deduced from written descriptions, archeological remains, and pictorial material. An "authentic" performance is particularly challenging in the re-creation of older music, whether from oral tradition, in which case it has typically undergone changes in the course of its transmission, or from notated repertoires that fell into obscurity as they were eclipsed by newer styles and tastes. The study of performance practice is an active and often controversial area of contemporary music scholarship.

Over the past 50 years, the performance of early music from the Western tradition has become increasingly the province of specialists trained in performance practices that have long been obsolete. For example, singers of medieval and Renaissance music cultivate a vocal style that is different from that employed in music of later periods, and instrumentalists learn techniques associated with playing period instruments, either old instruments that have been preserved or modern reproductions. Professional early music groups are usually led by scholar/performers devoted to the discovery and study of older repertory, and to seeking solutions to the many unanswered questions about the interpretation of early music. Many music schools, conservatories, and college music departments offer courses in the history and performance practice of early music and the opportunity to perform in early music ensembles. Churches, art galleries, museums, and small concert halls are favorite venues for live concerts of early music.

Likewise, groups of musicians and scholars have become devoted to the revival and preservation of a variety of older vernacular music traditions. Historical recordings have become a vital part of the process of re-creating performance practices and authentic style. For example, using commercial recordings from the 1920s and 1930s in conjunction with written scores and charts, contemporary jazz repertory bands have re-created the sounds of early New Orleans jazz and big band swing music. Field recordings of traditional ballads, blues, and hillbilly bands made during the Depression years fueled the urban folk music revival of the 1960s and early 1970s. Today an array of "ethnic" folk styles, ranging from Irish fiddling and Jewish klezmer to Caribbean and African drumming to Asian folk dance music are being studied and faithfully re-created for new audiences around the world. The advent of recording technology and new delivery systems (broadcast, cable, satellite, Internet, etc.) have collapsed time and space to make a panoply of world music performance practices and styles available to an ever expanding global audience.

Social Setting and Performance Rules

The relationship between the performers and audience members is highly dependent on the social setting in which a particular musical event takes place. The rules that govern proper performance will vary from setting to setting, and from culture to culture. In the western concert tradition, for example, the performers sit on a raised presidium stage which provides a spatial separation between them and their audience. Audience members are expected to sit in silent contemplation during the performance (cell phones off please!), clapping only when the conductor walks on stage, at the end of a piece and at the end of the concert (not in-between movements or after solos, except at the opera where applause and shouts of bravo, brava, and bravi are customary expressions of approval). At an African American gospel service, in contrast, the singers may leave the stage and walk/run/dance out among audience members who are expected to clap, stamp, and shout encouragement to the performers throughout a song. At a jazz club quiet talk is usually permissible, and audience members are expected to clap not only at the end of a piece but also after a particularly moving solo is played by one of the performers.

In many social settings audience members do more than sit and listen. At a wedding or at a dance club, for example, audience members dance in a designated space in front of the ensemble, and the musicians are expected to play an appropriate repertoire for the event and the indented audience. One expects a certain type of music and dancing at a rock or blues club, another at a salsa club, and another at a Jewish, Italian, or Greek wedding. Dancers may shout encouragement and make requests to the band, and musicians often watch the dancers to determine how long to keep a piece going, or whether to play a fast or slow piece next. In various Afro-Caribbean religious rituals the musicians drum and chant to call down the spirits to worshipers who dance and trance in special areas of the ceremony. In outdoor events like West Indian Carnival, the musicians and the dancers often merge into one dancing throng to the point where it is impossible to differentiate the performers from the audience members.

All musical performances are governed by rules that are setting and culture specific. The next time you plan to hear a live music performance, think about the expectations for performer and audience interaction that are appropriate for that particular setting. If you find yourself in an unfamiliar situation, be observant and see if you can determine the appropriate rules.

CHAPTER 4: EUROPEAN ART MUSIC: MIDDLE AGES THROUGH ROMANTIC

Middle Ages (ca. 450 to ca. 1450)

The period in the history of Western Europe, today called the Middle Ages, begins around 450 A.D. What had once been a vast empire dominated by Roman law and culture fell apart in consequence of a series of incursions by the Goths, Huns, and other "barbarian" tribes. Europe became a feudal society in which the majority of the population was peasants, or serfs. The landowners were noblemen who lived in tapestry-hung castles in walled villages, some of which are the antecedents of European cities of today. To fight the almost constant wars with each other, powerful lords raised their sons to be warriors, knights who pledged to follow codes of loyalty and chivalry. When not engaged in battles, these armored fighters participated in elaborate tournaments for the entertainment of the court. Knights also joined the crusades, multi-year Christian expeditions to the Middle East to recapture the Holy Land from Moslem rule.

As Christianity spread during the Middle Ages, great cathedrals were built across Europe as places of public worship, each presided over by a bishop appointed by the pope. Monasteries and convents were established as self-sufficient religious communities where monks and nuns lived in isolation from the outside world. At a time when the population was essentially illiterate, monasteries were centers of learning. Monks copied and illustrated religious manuscripts as well as books that preserved writings of Arabic and Greek scholars.

Monasteries have a special significance in the history of European music. The intoning of sacred texts, a practice the early Christians borrowed from other religions, was an important element of their liturgy. The chants sung in the services, some of them of ancient origin, were passed on through oral tradition, undoubtedly undergoing changes in the process. In order to bring some organization to this huge body of melodies, monks formulated principles for classifying the scales on which they were based, the church modes. They also experimented with methods of writing them down. Monophonic chants constituted the core of the repertory, but there were also practices of performing chants with one or more melodies added to them, an early form of polyphony. The system that the monks ultimately developed, essentially the staff of lines and spaces in use today, accomplished not only the exact fixing of the pitches of a melody, but allowed for the notation of two or more simultaneous melodies that graphically represented their relationship to one another. Observations about these relationships led to concepts of consonance and dissonance and to early rules for creating new music of two or more parts. What was originally intended as a mechanism for preserving existing music laid the foundations for Western theories of counterpoint and harmony. Those principles and practices made possible the composition of music of great textural complexity and are themselves among the major intellectual achievements in human history.

Historic Context

Fall of the Roman Empire around 450.

Rise of the Byzantine/Eastern Roman, Frankish/Western Roman, Persian, Moslem, and Turkish Empires.

Plague of 542–594 kills half the population of Europe.

Charlemagne (742–814) crowned Holy Roman Emperor, 800.

Viking shipbuilding flourishes ca. 900.

Heroic poem *Beowulf* ca. 1000.

Discovery of the Americas by Leif Eriksson ca. 1000.

First Crusade 1095–1099 followed by succession of crusades ending in 1291.

Signing of the Magna Carta, limiting the power of the English king, 1215.

Black Death 1347–1349 and 1361 kills a third of the population of Europe.

"Death of Knighthood" at Battle of Agincourt, 1415; French knights in armor are defeated by English armed with crossbows.

Joan of Arc burned at the stake, 1431.

Establishment of major European cities: Venice (ca. 450), Granada (ca. 750), Dublin (ca. 840), Leipzig (ca. 1015), Vienna (ca. 1220), Copenhagen (ca. 1040), Nuremberg (ca. 1050), Oslo (ca. 1050), Munich (ca. 1100), Moscow (ca. 1150), Belfast (ca. 1170), Heidelberg (ca. 1200), Liverpool (ca. 1200), Amsterdam (ca. 1200), Berlin (ca. 1230), Prague (ca. 1250), Stockholm (ca. 1250).

Spread of Christianity through Europe: Vatican Palace built ca. 500; Benedictine Order founded 529; Wales converted to Christianity ca. 550; Papacy of Gregory I 590–604; Parthenon in Rome consecrated as Church of S. Maria Rotunda, 609; Monastery of St. Gallen, Switzerland, founded 612; Gloucester Abbey founded 681; first canonization of saints 993; Iceland and Greenland converted to Christianity ca. 1000.

Building of cathedrals and basilicas: building of St. Sophia Basilica in Constantinople 532–537; Arles Cathedral founded ca. 600; St. Paul's Church, London, founded ca. 603; founding of Winchester Cathedral 685; Basilica of St. Mark, Venice (975–1094); consecration of Westminster Abbey (1065); Canterbury Cathedral (1070–1503); Chartres Cathedral 1134–1260; Verona Cathedral (1139–1187); Notre Dame Cathedral (1163–1235); Sainte-Chapelle, Paris (1246–1258); Cologne Cathedral, 1248–1880; Seville 1402.

Founding of universities: Salerno (850); Paris (1150); Oxford (1167); Bologna (1119); Siena (1203); Vicenza (1204); Salamanca (1217); Toulouse (1229); The Sorbonne (1254); Montpellier (1289); Lisbon (1290); Rome (1303); Grenoble (1339); Pisa (1338); Prague (1348); Vienna (1366); Heidelberg (1386); Cologne (1388).

Milestones in Music

Founding of Schola Cantorum by Pope Gregory in Rome, 600 AD.

Experiments in notation of pitch; first use of neumes, ca. 650.

Musica enchiriadis, treatise describing early polyphony (organum), ca. 870.

Emergence of staff notation as preferred system, ca. 900.

Organ with 400 pipes at Winchester Cathedral, ca. 980.

Advances in notation of rhythm, 13th century.

Earliest preserved examples of composed music of two or more independent melodies ca. 850–900.

Earliest theories of consonance and dissonance, 12th century.

Treatises describing advances in notation of rhythm ca. 1280 and ca. 1320.

Musical Genres

Chant, monophonic settings of texts used in services of the early Christian church.

Monophonic settings of secular poems, often about courtly love, by poet/musicians called troubadours and trouveres.

Polyphonic settings of sacred and secular texts for two or three parts, sometimes with one of the parts a preexistent melody, such as a chant.

Monophonic dances.

Major Figures in Music

Leonin (ca. 1135–1201): composer and compiler of early polyphony consisting of two melodic lines, active at Notre Dame Cathedral in Paris.

Perotin (1180–ca. 1207): successor of Leonin at Notre Dame, continued development of polyphony, mainly consisting of three melodic lines.

Guillaume de Machaut (ca. 1300–1377): French cleric, poet, and musician; composer of sacred and secular works, mostly consisting of three melodic lines.

Francesco Landini (ca. 1325–1397): Italian composer of secular songs, mostly consisting of three melodic lines.

Guillaume Dufay (ca. 1400–1474): Netherlandish composer of secular and sacred works of three or four melodic lines.

Other Historic Figures

St. Augustine (354–430): early Christian thinker and writer.

Boethius (ca. 480–524): Roman statesman and philosopher, author of *The Consolations of Philosophy* and *De institutione musica*, a treatise on numerical properties of musical sounds and the relationship between mathematical proportions and human morality.

Mohammed (590–632): founder of Islam.

Avicenna (980–1037): Islamic philosopher, scientist, and physician.

Anselm (1033–1109): Christian philosopher; propounded the ontological argument for God's existence.

Averroes (1126–1198): Islamic philosopher and commentator on Aristotle.

Maimonides (1125–1204): Jewish philosopher; author of *Guide to the Perplexed*.

Marco Polo (1254–1324): Venetian traveler to China 1271–1295.

Thomas Aquinas (ca. 1225–1274): Catholic scholar and philosopher.

Dante Alighieri (1265–1321): Italian poet, author of *The Divine Comedy* (1307), a cosmology of medieval Catholicism.

Giotto (ca. 1268–1337): Italian painter; frescoes of biblical scenes in churches of Florence and Padua.

Francesco Petrarca (Petrarch) (1304–1374): Italian poet; sonnets of idealized love.

Boccacio (1313–1375): Italian poet, author of the *Decameron* (1353), 100 witty and often bawdy allegorical tales set in the time of the Black Death in Florence.

Geoffrey Chaucer (ca. 1340–1400): English poet and writer, author of *Canterbury Tales* (1387), stories of courtly romance, deceit, and greed related by 30 people from different segments of English medieval society on a pilgrimage to Canterbury Cathedral.

Jan van Eyck (ca. 1390–1441): Flemish painter; domestic scenes painted in oils.

Renaissance (ca. 1450–1600)

The designation "Renaissance" dates from the 18th century and reflects the revival of interest in the classical civilizations of Greece and Rome that profoundly influenced the culture and thinking of the century and a half following the Middle Ages. The period is also called the Age of Humanism because of the emphasis on the nature, potential, and accomplishments of man in literature, art and music, science, and philosophy. The medieval approach to understanding the world, which was based on speculative systems of divine order and harmony, was supplanted by theories derived from scientific observation. Learning was highly valued and, through the invention of printing, became available to a wide population. Other important inventions are the telescope and instruments for navigation used by explorers such as Columbus and Magellan.

The Catholic Church remained an important institution during the Renaissance, but diminished in influence in consequence of the wealth and power of families such as the Medici of Florence and the Estes of Ferrara, whose courts became centers of culture, learning, and military might. The Reformation, which began with Martin Luther's criticisms of Church abuses, had its greatest impact in Germany. Other breakaway movements followed in France and Switzerland, as well as in England, where Henry VIII defied the authority of the pope and declared himself head of a new Anglican church. Wars between Catholics and Protestants are part of the history of many of the countries that broke with Rome.

In music and the other arts, patronage by royalty, who competed in maintaining splendid courts as well as chapels, spurred the development of secular forms of artistic expression.

Whether secular or sacred, Renaissance art, sculpture, and architecture embody the ideals of balance, clarity, and emotional restraint that characterized the classicism of the Greeks. In music, where no ancient models survived, that aesthetic found expression in a style that evolved from concepts of consonance and dissonance developed in the Middle Ages but with new emphasis on harmonious sonorities. The predominant texture consisted of soprano, alto, tenor, and bass voice parts creating a highly contrapuntal web in which the lines diverge, converge, cross, echo, and imitate each other, sometimes with great rhythmic independence, sometimes moving together in the manner of a hymn. In setting religious texts, composers strove for an atmosphere of serenity and spirituality, in the setting of secular texts, for vivid representation of words and images. Instrumental music continued to be of secondary importance to composers, whose approach to writing for instruments was usually the same as that for voices. For example, published collections of dances required unspecified instruments of soprano, alto, tenor, and bass range—in essence vocal pieces without words. Some composers, however, began to explore shaping musical material in ways that exploited the unique features of the instruments on which it would be performed.

Historic Context
End of Hundred Year's War between England and France, ca. 1450.
Capture of Constantinople, capital of the Eastern church, by Turks, 1453.
Johannes Gutenberg (ca. 1396–1468) inventor of printing in Europe, prints Bible from movable type, ca, 1454.
Building of Palazzo Pitti, Florence, 1460.
Start of the Spanish Inquisition, 1481.
Tudor dynasty in England, 1485–1603.
Christopher Columbus first voyage to the New World 1492; last voyage 1501–1504.
Beginning of printing of the *Aldrines*, series of Greek classics of Aristotle, Aristophanes, et al., 1495.
Beginning of postal service, between Vienna and Brussels, 1500.
Coronation of Henry VIII as King of England, 1509.
Pineapples imported into Europe, 1514.
Martin Luther's ninety-five theses nailed to church door at Wittenberg, 1517; beginning of the Reformation.

Coffee introduced to Europe 1517.

License granted to import African slaves to Spanish colonies in New World, 1518.

Cortes brings horses from Spain to North America, 1518.

Ferdinand Magellan (1480–1521) sets off to circumnavigate the globe, 1519.

Founding of Royal Library of France at Fontainebleau, 1520.

Chocolate brought from Mexico to Spain, 1520.

Martin Luther begins translation of Bible from Latin to German, 1521, completed 1534.

Manufacture of silk introduced to France, 1521.

Discovery of New York harbor and Hudson River by Giovanni da Verrazano, 1524.

Outbreaks of plague in England, 1528.

Henry VIII breaks with Rome and establishes Anglican Church, 1534.

Building of St. Basil's, Moscow, 1534–1561.

Collected works of Cicero published in Venice, 1537.

Hernando de Soto discovers Mississippi River, 1541.

Council of Trent (1545–1563): meeting of church leaders called by Pope Paul III to address abuses in Catholic Church.

Beginning of building of the Louvre, Paris, 1546.

Tobacco brought from America to Spain, 1555.

Coronation of Elizabeth I as Queen of England, 1559.

Tulips introduced to Europe from Near East, 1561.

Outbreak of plague in Europe, over 20,000 die in London, 1563.

Two million Indians die in South America from typhoid fever introduced by Europeans, 1567.

St. Bartholomew's Day massacre of 2,000 Huguenots (French Protestants) in Paris, 1572.

Outbreak of plague in Italy, 1575.

Defeat of the Spanish Armada by the English, 1588.

Outbreak of plague in London kills 15,000, 1592.

Publication of Mercator's atlas, 1595.

Tomatoes introduced in England, 1596.

Dutch opticians invent the telescope, 1600.

Milestones in Music

First printed collection of polyphonic music by Ottaviano Petrucci, Venice, 1501; in 1520s and 1530s music printing houses founded in London, Paris, Venice, Rome, Nuremberg, and Antwerp.

Publication of tutors on composing music and playing instruments.

Founding of first conservatories of music in Naples and Venice, 1537.

Early development of the violin, 1550s.

Florentine Camerata meets in the home of Giovanni Bardi and speculates about the correct performance of Greek drama leading to the creation of *recitative* style singing and the invention of *opera*, 1573 to c. 1590.

Musical Genres

Motet: setting of Latin sacred text; principal performance medium a cappella chorus of soprano, alto, tenor bass; texture of imitative counterpoint. Josquin des Prez set the model for the Renaissance motet.

Mass: setting of texts of the Mass Ordinary; principal performance medium a cappella chorus of soprano, alto, tenor bass; texture of imitative counterpoint. Almost all Renaissance composers wrote masses.

Madrigal: setting of secular text; principal performance medium a cappella chorus of soprano, alto, tenor bass; texture of imitative counterpoint; main secular genre in Italy and England; use of word painting to illustrate text images.

Chanson: a cappella setting of secular text; principal performance medium a cappella chorus of soprano, alto, tenor, bass; principal secular genre in France.

Chorale: setting of German sacred text; introduced by Martin Luther for congregational singing.

Canzona: instrumental adaptation of the chanson. Giovanni Gabrieli's canzones were probably composed for religious celebrations at St. Mark's in Venice.

Dances: instrumental works to accompany dancing, often paired as a slow dance with gliding movements followed by a faster dance with leaping movements.

Major Figures in Music

Johannes Ockeghem (ca. 1420–1497): composer of sacred and secular music, active in Antwerp; teacher of many early Renaissance composers.

Josquin des Prez (ca. 1440–1521): Franco-Flemish composer; see Musician Biographies.

Giovanni Gabrieli: Italian composer; director of music at St. Mark's in Venice.

Giovanni Pierluigi da Palestrina (1525–1594): Italian composer of sacred and secular music; credited with introducing Counterreformation reforms following the Council of Trent; referred to by contemporaries as The Prince of Music.

William Byrd (1543–1623): English composer of sacred and secular vocal music and works for the keyboard.

Tomas Luis de Victoria (1548–1611): Spanish composer of sacred music.

Other Historic Figures

Donatello (1368–1466): Italian sculptor; works depicting religious subjects for churches and chapels in Florence, Siena, Padua, Venice.

Filippo Brunelleschi (1372–1446): Italian architect, designer of dome of Santa Maria del Fiore in Florence.

Fra Angelico (1387–1455): Italian painter; frescoes of New Testament scenes in Florence and the Vatican.

Johann Gutenberg (ca. 1396–1468): German printer; first Bible printed using movable type.

Fra Filippo Lippi (ca. 1406–1469): Italian painter, especially esteemed for his frescoes and altarpieces.

Hans Memling (1433–1484): Dutch painter active in Bruges; altarpieces, portraits notable for attention to facial detail; *Adoration of the Magi, The Last Judgment*.

Sandro Botticelli (1444–1510): Italian painter; *Birth of Venus*.

Lorenzo de' Medici, "The Magnificent" (1449–1492): Florentine aristocrat and important patron of artists, including Leonardo da Vinci.

Christopher Columbus (1451–1506): Italian explorer; voyages to the "new world" 1492-1504.

Leonardo da Vinci (1452–1519): Italian painter, sculptor, architect, engineer, inventor, philosopher; *The Last Supper, Mona Lisa*; scientific drawings.

Erasmus of Rotterdam (1465–1536): humanist, theologian, and writer on free will, superstition, religious orthodoxy; credited with the adage "In the land of the blind the one-eyed man is king."

Niccolo Machiavelli (1469–1527): Italian writer and politician; author of *The Prince*, an examination of the nature and exercise of political power.

Nicolaus Copernicus (1473–1543): Polish astronomer; observations on movement of planets and stars.

Michelangelo Buonarroti (1475–1564): Italian sculptor, painter, poet, architect; *Pietá*, ceiling and fresco of *The Last Judgment* in the Sistine Chapel of the Vatican; chief architect of St. Peter's, Rome.

Titian (1477–1576): Italian painter of portraits and landscapes, mythological and religious subjects, active in Venice and Spain.

Thomas More (1478–1535): English lawyer, statesman, and humanist; executed for his opposition to Henry VIII's establishing Church of England with himself as its head; author of *Utopia* which describes an ideal, imaginary nation.

Martin Luther (1483–1546): German religious reformer, founder of Protestanism; translated *The Bible* into German.

Henry VIII (1491–1547): king of England, 1509 to 1547; established Church of England in defiance of Rome's refusal to grant him a divorce.

Jean Calvin (1509–1564): founder of Calvinism, form of Protestantism adopted by the Pilgrims.

Tintoretto (1518–1594): Italian painter; scenes from the life of Christ and of the Virgin Mary in the Scuolo San Rocco in Venice; also painted mythological scenes and portraits.

Elizabeth I (1533–1603): queen of England 1558 to 1603, referred to as England's Golden Age; a gifted and well educated monarch, lover of theater, music, and dance.

El Greco (1541–1614): Spanish-Greek painter; paintings and altarpieces of mystical intensity in Toledo; also portraits; *View of Toledo* in New York's Metropolitan Museum.

Torquato Tasso (1544–1595): Italian poet; author of *Jerusalem Delivered* about the Third Crusade.

Miguel de Cervantes (1547–1616): Spanish writer, author of *Don Quixote*.

Francis Bacon (1561–1626): English lawyer, politician, and philosopher at the court of Elizabeth I.

William Shakespeare (1564–1616): English playwright and poet; author of *Romeo and Juliet, Merchant of Venice, Hamlet, Macbeth*, numerous history plays, sonnets.

Christopher Marlowe (1564–1593): English playwright, author of *Tamburlaine* and *Dr. Faustus*.

Galileo Galilei (1564–1642): Italian scientist, experiments in the study of gravity and astronomy; in 1633 condemned by the Catholic Church to lifelong imprisonment for defending Copernicus's theory that the earth revolves around the sun.

Baroque (ca. 1600–1750)

Many of the historic events in Europe during the 17th and early 18th centuries are extensions of forces that shaped and defined the Renaissance. The explorations of the 16th century were followed by the establishment of more and more colonies in the New World. In the sphere of intellectual activity, the scientific methodologies and discoveries of Copernicus and Galileo laid the foundations for the work of Kepler and Newton, and the philosophers Descartes, Spinoza, and Locke embraced the Renaissance pursuit of truth through reason. Religious conflicts engendered by the Reformation continued to erupt throughout the 17th century. In the area that is now Germany, tensions between Protestants and Catholics following the Reformation ignited a catastrophic Thirty Years War, during the course of which half the population died. The history of England is also a violent one, with such bloody deeds as the beheading of Mary Queen of Scots and Charles I, both Catholics, and the posthumous hanging and dismemberment of Oliver Cromwell, a commoner and Puritan who became England's Lord Protector during the Commonwealth period. The powers of the absolute monarch reached new heights in France, whose citizens were heavily taxed to support Louis XIV and the 20,000 courtiers who lived at the extravagant palace he had built for himself at Versailles.

These were some of the contexts in which artists worked during the approximately 150-year period of the Baroque. As in the Renaissance, popes, cardinals, monarchs, and members of the aristocracy continued to use art as a symbol of power and wealth. But artists and musicians also created works for a wider public. The art, architecture, and music they created exhibit features that are characteristic of romantic expression—intense emotion, flamboyance, and dynamic movement. For subjects, painters and sculptors were drawn to dramatic moments from mythology, ancient history, and the Bible, which they depicted with elaborate decoration, vivid color, and bold use of light and shadow. They also portrayed scenes from everyday life that were displayed in the homes of the rising middle class. Architecture, often grandiose in scale, employed sweeping lines, high domes, columns, and statues, all overlaid with ornamental detail. The taste for dramatic expression in conjunction with the opening of public concert halls created a supportive climate for the emergence of opera and oratorio and of new instrumental genres independent of vocal music such as the sonata, concerto, and suite. In their pursuit of dramatic intensity, composers introduced strongly contrasting effects—between loud and soft, between soloist and large group, between voices and instruments—and developed a vocabulary of devices that associated particular keys, meters, rhythmic figures, and instruments with specific emotional states, such as anger, love, joy, and grief.

Historic Context

Founding of Dutch East India Company, 1602.
Founding of Sante Fe, New Mexico, 1605.
Founding of Jamestown, Virginia, 1607.
Dutch East India Company ships tea from China shipped to Europe, 1609.
Discovery of Hudson Bay by Henry Hudson, 1610.
King James Bible published, 1611; first authorized version of the Bible in English.
Tobacco planted in Virginia, 1612.
Thirty Years War in Germany, 1618–1648; almost half the population dies due to war, famine, and plague.
Discovery of circulation of the blood by William Harvey, 1619.
First African slaves in North America arrive in Virginia, 1619.
Pilgrims arrive in Massachusetts, 1620.
Dutch West Indies Company purchases Manhattan Island from native Indians; colony of New Amsterdam founded, 1626.

Founding of colony of Massachusetts, 1629.
Founding of Harvard College, 1636.
Bay Psalm Book, oldest surviving printed book in America, 1640.
English Commonwealth, 1649–1660, under leadership of Oliver Cromwell.
Restoration of English monarchy, 1660.
Founding of Academic Royale de Danse by Louis XIV, 1661.
Louis XIV begins building of Versailles, 1662.
Plague in London kills 68,000, 1665.
Great Fire of London, 1666.
Founding of the College of William and Mary, Virginia, 1692.
Inoculation against small pox introduced in England, 1717.
Frederick the Great introduces freedom of the press and freedom of worship in Prussia, 1740.

Milestones in Music

Guilio Caccini, *Nuove musiche*, 1601; collection of songs for solo voice and instrumental accompaniment, establishing a texture used throughout the baroque period.
Performance of Monteverdi's *Orfeo*, 1607, considered first important opera.
Encyclopedia of music by German composer Michael Praetorius, 1620.
First public opera house, Teatro San Cassiano, opens in Venice, 1637.
Founding of Academic Royale des Operas, Paris, 1669.
Opening of Paris Opera, 1671.
First German opera house opens in Hamburg, 1678.
Vivaldi appointed maestro di violono at orphanage for girls in Venice, 1703.
Invention of the pianoforte by Bartolomeo Cristofori, Italian harpsichord maker, 1709.
Handel settles permanently in London, 1711.
Bach accepts position as cantor of St. Thomas Church, Leipzig, 1723.
First public concerts in Paris, Concerts Spirituels, 1725.
First performance of Handel's *Messiah*, Dublin, 1742.

Musical Genres

Opera: drama set to music for singers and instruments and acted on the stage with sets and costumes. Monteverdi is generally considered to be the most important composer of the early Baroque, Handel of the late Baroque.
Oratorio: a story, usually religious, set to music but performed without staging. Oratorio, like opera, originated in Italy. Handel is the most important oratorio composer of the late Baroque.
Cantata: multiple movement vocal work on a pastoral or religious text. Bach composed over 300 cantatas for performance on Sundays throughout the church year.
Concerto: instrumental composition that pits one or more soloists against the orchestra. Vivaldi was a major figure in the standardization of the design and character of the solo concerto.
Fugue: a polyphonic composition, usually for four voice parts, based on one theme or subject that is developed in an imitative texture. Bach's many fugues sum up the art of fugal writing.
Sonata: in the Baroque period, an instrumental chamber work for one or two melody instruments and continuo accompaniment. Arcangelo Corelli's sonatas for two violins and continuo are considered classic examples of the genre.
Suite: collection of instrumental dance movements of different character and often national origin. Thus, the allemande from Germany, courante from France, gigue (jig) from the British Isles. Suites were composed for the harpsichord and for chamber and orchestral ensembles. Couperin and Bach made major contributions to this repertory.

Major Figures in Music

Claudio Monteverdi (1567–1643): Italian composer of *Orfeo* of 1607, which is generally regarded as the first great opera; maestro di cappella at St. Mark's Venice 1613–1643.
Nicola Amati (1596–1684): Italian violin maker.
Jean-Baptiste Lully (1632–1675): Italian-born composer who dominated music at court of Louis XIV.

Antonio Stradivari (1644–1737): Italian violin maker.

Arcangelo Corelli (1653–1677): Italian composer of instrumental sonatas and concertos for violin.

Henry Purcell (1659–1695): English composer of songs, religious choral music, instrumental and theatrical works, including the opera *Dido and Aeneas*, 1689.

Francois Couperin (1668–1733): French composer and keyboard player at the court of Louis XIV and XV.

Antonio Vivaldi (1675–1741): Italian composer and seminal figure in the development of the solo concerto; see Musician Biographies.

Jean Philippe Rameau (1683–1764): French theorist and composer of operas and keyboard suites.

Johann Sebastian Bach (1685–1750): North German composer and cantor of Leipzig, Germany; see Musician Biographies.

George Frederick Handel (1685–1759): North German composer of *The Messiah*, among other oratorios; see Musician Biographies.

Other Historic Figures

Johannes Kepler (1571–1630): German astronomer; laws explaining planetary movement around the sun.

Michelangelo da Caravaggio (1571–1610): Italian painter; *Conversion of St. Paul, Death of the Virgin*.

Peter Paul Rubens (1577–1640): Flemish painter; *Elevation of the Cross, The Lion Hunt*.

Franz Hals (1580–1666): Dutch painter; favorite subjects were merchants, ministers, common folk.

Thomas Hobbes (1588–1679): English philosopher; materialist who advocated authoritarian social system; author of *Leviathan*.

Rene Descartes (1596–1650): French mathematician and philosopher of dualism; "cogito ergo sum"; inventor of analytic geometry.

Giovanni Bernini (1598–1680): Italian sculptor; *David, Ecstacy of St. Terese*, design of piazza of St. Peter's, Rome.

Oliver Cromwell (1599–1658): English general and statesman; Puritan and political leader during the Commonwealth period.

Diego Velasquez (1599–1660): Spanish painter of portraits, religious and historical subjects.

Anthony Van Dyck (1599–1641): Dutch painter; portraits of English nobility at court of Charles I.

Rembrandt van Rijn (1606–1669): Dutch painter; favored common people as subjects; *The Night Watch*, self-portraits.

John Milton (1608–1674): English poet; *Paradise Lost, Paradise Regained*.

John Dryden (1631–1700): English poet, literary, playwright of satirical dramas.

Jan Vermeer (1632–1675): Dutch painter; portraits and everyday scenes; *Girl with a Pearl Earring*.

John Locke (1632–1704): English philosopher; enlightenment thinker and empiricist.

Christopher Wren (1632–1723): English architect; St. Paul's Cathedral, London.

Baruch Spinoza (1632–1677): Dutch philosopher; enlightenment thinker.

Louis XIV (1638–1715): king of France 1642 to 1715, known as Le Roi du Soleil (The Sun King); quintessential absolute monarch; builder of Versailles.

Jean Racine (1639–1699): French poet and playwright; *Phedre*.

Isaac Newton (1642–1727): English mathematician and philosopher; experiments on gravitation, motion, and optics.

Gottfried Wilhelm von Leibnitz (1646–1716): German rationalist philosopher, mathematician, historian, and jurist.

Jonathan Swift (1667–1745): English writer and satirist; *Gulliver's Travels*.

Peter the Great (1672–1725): becomes Czar of Russia, 1689.

George Berkeley (1685–1753): empiricist philosopher and bishop; propounded Idealism against Locke's common-sense Realism.

Classical (Enlightenment Period) (ca. 1750–ca. 1820)

The term classical, when used in the context of works of art, refers to features such proportion and symmetry that characterize the sculpture and architecture of ancient Greece and Rome and also the art of subsequent periods that display those features. Classicists embrace the notion of universal ideals of beauty and strive in art to achieve universality through the representation of ideal forms.

It is for this reason that the period that followed the Baroque, when the flamboyance and drama were supplanted by emotional restraint and formal balance and symmetry, is called Classical. The 18th century is also called the Enlightenment Period, because of the ideals of reason, objectivity, and scientific knowledge found in the writings of Diderot, Voltaire, and Lessing that permeated all aspects of European society and culture. Thomas Jefferson, John Adams, and Ben Franklin are among the Americans who shared the belief in human progress and natural rights, that is, the rights of the individual as opposed to the rights of the state, as embodied in a monarch. These ideas led to the American Revolution, then the French Revolution, with its slogan "Liberty, Equality, Fraternity."

Both the aesthetics of classicism and the Enlightenment world view shaped the art of the second half of the 18th and early 19th centuries. As in the Renaissance, architects once again found inspiration in the proportion and grace of Greek and Roman temples. Robert Burns's poems in Scottish dialect, Jane Austen's novels about life in a country village, and Schiller's plays about aspirations for freedom and brotherhood are testaments to enlightenment notions of the dignity and worth of the common man.

In music, composers of the early classical period discarded complex textures, learned compositional techniques such as fugal imitation, and grandeur in favor of transparent textures, a single melody supported by a subordinate accompaniment, and somewhat superficial sentiments. In the mature classical style of Haydn, Mozart, and early Beethoven, counterpoint, processes of rigorous development, and depth of expression reappear, but in the context of classical ideals of clarity, proportion, and refined taste. Important developments during the period include expansion of the orchestra to thirty or forty players, improvements in the mechanisms of instruments, especially the piano, and ever greater public support through concerts and publication of music.

Historic Context
Building of Independence Hall, Philadelphia, 1731–1751.
First playhouse opens in New York, 1750.
King's College (Columbia University) founded 1754.
Moscow University founded 1755.
First public restaurant opens in Paris, 1770.
New York Hospital founded, 1771.
Boston Tea Party in protest against tea tax, 1773.
Louis XVI assumes throne of France, 1774.
Beginning of the American Revolution; Second Continental Congress in Philadelphia; George
    Washington made commander of American forces, 1775.
U.S. Declaration of Independence, 1776.
Adam Smith (1723–1790) publishes *The Wealth of Nations*, 1776.
American Academy of Sciences founded in Boston, 1780.
Bank of North American established in Philadelphia, 1782.
Great Britain recognizes independence of American colonies, 1783.
U.S. Constitution signed in Philadelphia, 1878.
French Revolution, 1789.
U.S. Bill of Rights ratified, 1791.
Louis XVI executed, 1793; beginning of Reign of Terror in France.
Building of U.S. Capitol in Washington begins, 1793.

Eli Whitney (1765–1825) invents the cotton gin, 1793.

Slavery abolished in French colonies, 1794.

Napoleon crowned emperor, 1804; King of Italy, 1805; King of Spain, 1808.

England prohibits slave trade, 1807.

War of 1812: Napoleon invades Russia; only 20,000 of his 550,000-member army survive.

Louisiana becomes a U.S. state, 1812.

Mexico declares independence from Spain, 1813; becomes a republic, 1823.

Napoleon abdicates and is exiled to Elba, 1814; returns to France, 1815; defeated in Battle of Waterloo by Wellington, 1815.

Simon Bolivar establishes Venezuela as independent government, 1817.

Chile proclaims independence, 1818.

Working day for juveniles limited to 12 hours in England, 1819.

Brazil becomes independent of Portugal, 1822.

Milestones in Music

Mozart's first tour of Europe as six-year-old child prodigy, 1762.

Handel's *Messiah* first performed in New York, 1770.

Opening of La Scala opera house in Milan, 1778.

English piano maker John Broadwood patents piano pedals, 1783.

Charles Burney's *History of Music*, 1789.

Founding of the Paris Conservatoire, 1795.

Founding of Prague Conservatory, 1811.

Musical Genres

Concerto: instrumental work pitting a soloist against the orchestra. Mozart wrote a number of piano concertos featuring himself as the soloist.

Piano sonata: multi-movement work for solo piano. All composers of the period contributed to this genre.

String quartet: four-movement work for two violins, viola, and cello favored by Haydn, who established the grouping as the premiere chamber medium.

Symphony: four-movement work for orchestra. Haydn composed 104 symphonies, Mozart 41, and Beethoven 9.

Opera: as in the baroque period, a drama set to music and staged. Mozart was the most important opera composer of the period.

Major Figures in Music

Franz Josef Haydn (1632–1809): Viennese composer; see Musician Biographies.

Wolfgang Amadeus Mozart (1756–1791): Austrian composer; see Musician Biographies.

Ludwig van Beethoven (1770–1827): German late classical/early romantic composer; see Musician Biographies.

Other Historic Figures

Jean Antoine Watteau (1684–1764): French painter; *Embarkation for the Isle of Cythera*.

Voltaire (1694–1778): French writer and philosopher; champion of individual liberties and critic of organized religion.

Benjamin Franklin (1706–1790): American statesman and inventor; Founding Father of the United States; publisher of Pennsylvania Gazette; Ambassador to France.

Linnaeus (1707–1778): Swedish botanist; creator of scientific classification system for plants and animals.

David Hume (1711–1776): Scottish philosopher and historian, proponent of empiricism.

Jean-Jacques Rousseau (1712–1778): French philosopher; his ideas of liberty and equality taken up during French Revolution.

Frederick the Great (1712–1796): King of Prussia; enlightened monarch who inaugurated freedom of the press and worship; accomplished flutist who employed one of J. S. Bach's sons.

Denis Diderot (1713–1784): French philosopher; chief editor of *Encyclopedie*.

Adam Smith (1723–1790): Scottish economist and philosopher; author of *The Wealth of Nations*.

Joshua Reynolds (1723–1792): English portrait painter.

Immanuel Kant (1724–1804): German philosopher of metaphysics and epistemology; author of *Critique of Pure Reason*.

Thomas Gainsborough (1727–1788): English portrait painter of fashionable society and children; *Blue Boy*.

James Cook (1728–1779): English navigator and explorer of the Pacific.

Catherine the Great (1729–1796): czarina of Russia.

Gotthold Ephraim Lessing (1729–1781): German dramatist, critic, and philosopher.

George Washington (1732–1799): Revolutionary War general; first president of the United States.

Jean Honore Fragonard (1732–1806): French portrait painter.

John Adams (1735–1826): U.S. Founding Father and second president of the United States.

James Watt (1736–1819): Scottish inventor of the steam engine.

Thomas Jefferson (1743–1743): U.S. Founding Father, author of the Declaration of Independence, president of the United States, 1801 to 1809; lawyer, architect, statesman.

Francisco de Goya (1746–1828): Spanish painter; portraits of royalty; other subjects include inhumanity of war.

Jeremy Bentham (1748–1832): Utilitarian philosopher.

Jacques-Louis David (1748–1825): French painter.

Johann Wolfgang von Goethe (1749–1832): German poet, novelist, playwright, and statesman; author of *The Sorrows of Young Werther* and *Faust*.

Simon Bolivar (1758–1830): Latin American soldier and statesman; the "George Washington of South America;" major figure in independence from Spain for Bolivia, Panama, Colombia, Ecuador, Peru, and Venezuela.

Robert Burns (1759–1796): Scottish poet who wrote in the Scots language; *Auld Lang Syne*.

Johann von Schiller (1759–1805): German poet, playwright, and historian; author of poem used by Beethoven in his Symphony #9.

Napoleon Bonaparte (1769–1821): Corsican-born general, emperor of France, 1804 to 1814.

Georg Wilhelm Friedrich Hegel (1770–1831): German philosopher; writings on the history of philosophy and the philosophy of history, religion, and aesthetics.

Jane Austen (1775–1817): English novelist; author of *Pride and Prejudice, Emma, Persuasion, Mansfield Park*.

Romantic (ca. 1820–1900)

In many respects, the social and political history of 19th century Europe and the United States is a continuation of trends and movements rooted in the previous century: secularization, industrialization, democratization. But the way in which artists perceived, interpreted, and expressed the world was informed by a romantic aesthetic. As a general descriptive, romantic is applied to literature, visual arts, and music that emphasize imagination over objective observation, intense emotion over reason, freedom and spontaneity over order and control, individual over universal experience. The romantics of the 19th century sought inspiration in nature (poetry of Wordsworth, paintings of Constable and Turner), mythology and folklore (stories of E. T. A. Hoffmann), and the past (Keats, *Ode on a Grecian Urn*; Dumas, *The Three Musketeers*). They idolized tragic heroic figures (Sir Walter Scott's novel *Ivanhoe*), and the artist as visionary (Walt Whitman, "I celebrate myself, and sing myself"). And they were fascinated by subjects associated with dreams (Goya's *The Dream of Reason*), oppression, injustice, and political struggle (novels of Dickens, Victor Hugo's *Les Miserable*), the macabre (stories of Edgar Allen Poe), and death (poems of Emily Dickinson). The lives of many romantics were marked by the restlessness, longing, and unhappy love relationships they depicted through their art (the English poets Byron and Shelley).

Music was in a number of respects the perfect romantic art form. In the words of the composer Franz Liszt, "Music embodies feeling without forcing it to contend and combine with thought..." Music was used as a vehicle for expression of personal emotion, for awakening nationalistic aspirations, and for the display of virtuosity. Composers continued to use genres they inherited from past, such as the symphony, concerto, piano sonata, and opera, but also developed repertories particularly associated with the 19th century, such as the art song and instrumental program music. Whatever the form, romantic composers spoke a musical language infused with poetic lyricism, harmonic complexity, and dramatic contrasts. The requirements of their orchestral scores led to the expansion of the orchestra, both in size, to eighty or more players, and in its palette of instrumental colors through the addition of trombones and tubas, piccolo and contrabassoon, harp, cymbals, triangle, and a variety of drums. The concept of what constituted a single work encompassed the extremes from short, intimate songs and piano miniatures of Schubert and Schumann intended to be performed in intimate surroundings, to the operas of Wagner and symphonies of the late romantic written for large concert halls and demanding enormous performing resources.

Historic Context

Death of Napoleon I, 1821.
Mexico becomes a republic, 1823; slavery is abolished, 1829.
Slave revolt in Virginia led by Nat Turner, 1831.
Charles Darwin's expedition to South America, New Zealand, Australia, 1831–1836.
Anti-Slavery Society founded in Boston, 1832.
Abolition of slavery in British Empire, 1833.
Public demonstration of the telegraphy by Samuel Morse, 1837.
Vulcanization of rubber by American inventor Charles Goodyear, 1839.
Invention of the bicycle by Scottish inventor Kirkpatrick Macmillan, 1839.
Texas and Florida become U.S. states, 1845.
Founding of Smithsonian Institution, Washington, D.C., 1846.
Potato famine in Ireland, 1846.
First U.S. women's rights convention in Seneca Falls, N.Y., 1848.
Marx and Engels issue *The Communist Manifesto*, 1848.
First California gold rush, 1848.
California becomes U.S. state, 1850.

Continuous stitch sewing machine invented by Isaac Singer, 1851.

Paris World's Fair, 1855; subsequent fairs in London, 1862; Vienna, 1873; Philadelphia, 1876; Paris, 1878; Melbourne, 1880; Moscow, 1882; Amsterdam, 1883; Chicago, 1893, Brussels, 1897; Paris, 1900.

Construction of Suez Canal, 1859–1869.

Victor Emmanuel II named King of Italy by Garibaldi, 1860.

Lincoln elected sixteenth president of the United States, 1860.

U.S. Civil War, 1861–1865.

Speed of light measured by Foucault, 1862.

Lincoln issues Emancipation Proclamation; Gettysburg Address, 1863.

Thirteenth Amendment to U.S. Constitution abolishes slavery, 1865.

Alfred Nobel invents dynamite, 1866.

Russia sells Alaska to United States, 1867.

P. T. Barnum opens his circus "The Greatest Show in Earth," in Brooklyn, 1871.

Brooklyn Bridge opened, 1872.

Republic proclaimed in Spain, 1873.

First Impressionist exhibit, Paris, 1874.

Alexander Graham Bell invents the telephone, 1876.

Thomas Edison invents the phonograph, 1877.

Cholera vaccine discovered by Pasteur, 1880.

New York streets first lit by electric lights, 1880.

Tuskegee Institute founded by Booker T. Washington, 1881.

Pasteur invents rabies vaccine, 1885.

Statue of Liberty is dedicated, 1886.

Manufacture of electric motor constructed by Nikola Tesla, 1888.

Henry Ford builds first car, 1893.

Invention of motion picture camera by August and Louis Lumiere, 1895.

First Nobel prizes are awarded, 1896.

Milestones in Music

Founding of Royal Academy of Music, London, 1822.

Improvements in piano mechanism by French maker Erard, 1823.

Patent of the saxophone by Belgian instrument maker Adolphe Sax, 1841.

Founding of piano firm Steinway and Sons, New York, 1853.

New York Symphony gives its first public concert, 1858.

Metropolitan Opera House opens in New York, 1883.

First magnetic sound recordings, 1899.

Musical Genres

Art song: setting of a poetic text, usually for voice and piano. Schubert and Schumann were both masters of the art song.

Concerto: work for instrumental soloist and orchestra with prominent display of virtuosity. The violinist Paganini and the pianist Liszt wrote concertos to show off their astonishing technical abilities.

Opera: as in previous periods, a drama set to music; heavy emphasis on bel canto ("beautiful singing") and vocal virtuosity. The operas of Verdi, Puccini, and Wagner are standard repertory of opera companies today.

Program symphony: orchestral work that musically depicts a story, images, events, or other nonmusical subjects. Beethoven's Pastoral Symphony, Berlioz's *Symphonie Fantastique*, nationalistic orchestral works of Smetana, and the tone poems of Liszt and Strauss exemplify this genre.

Symphony: as in the classical period, a large-scale work for orchestra. Symphonies by Schubert, Schumann, Mendelssohn, Brahms, Tchaikovsky, Dvorak, and Mahler are staples of the orchestral repertory.

Major Figures in Music

Ludwig van Beethoven (1770–1827): German late classical/early romantic composer; see Musician Biographies.

Nicolo Paganini (1782–1840): Italian composer and violin virtuoso.

Franz Schubert (1797–1828): Austrian composer; see Musician Biographies.

Hector Berlioz (1803–1869): French composer.

Frederic Chopin (1810–1849): Polish-born composer and pianist.

Robert Schumann (1810–1856): German composer.

Franz Liszt (1811–1886): Hungarian-born composer and piano virtuoso.

Giuseppe Verdi (1813–1901): Italian opera composer; see Musician Biographies.

Richard Wagner (1813–1883): German opera composer.

Clara Wieck Schumann (1819–1896): German pianist; see Musician Biographies.

Bedrick Smetana (1824–1884): Czech nationalist composer.

Stephen Foster (1826–1864): American songwriter.

Johannes Brahms (1833–1897): German composer.

Modest Mussorgsky (1839–1881): Russian composer.

Peter Illich Tchaikovsky (1840–1893): Russian composer.

Antonin Dvorak (1841–1904): Czech composer; see Musician Biographies.

Giacomo Puccini (1858–1924): Italian opera composer; see Musician Biographies.

Gustav Mahler (1860–1911): German composer.

Claude Debussy (1862–1918): French impressionist composer.

Other Historic Figures

Francisco de Goya (1746–1828): Spanish painter; portraits of royalty; other subjects include inhumanity of war.

William Blake (1757–1827): English poet and artist; author of *Songs of Innocence*; illustrator of the Bible and works by Dante and Shakespeare.

William Wordsworth (1770–1850): English poet; *Lyrical Ballads* anthology; *Tintern Abbey, The Prelude.*

Walter Scott (1771–1832): Scottish poet and historical novelist; *Ivanhoe, Rob Roy, The Lady of the Lake.*

Joseph Turner (1775–1851): English landscape painter; subjects include London, scenes at sea, Venice; *The Grand Canal Venice* at Metropolitan Museum of Art in New York.

E.T.A. Hoffmann (1776–1822): German composer and writer; collections of folk tales; story enacted in Tchaikovsky's *Nutcracker.*

Clemens Brentano (1778–1842): German author and poet.

Lord Byron (1788–1824): English poet; his peripatetic wanderings and rebellious character inspired the concept of the"Byronic hero;" *Childe Harold's Pilgrimage.*

Arthur Schopenhauer (1788–1860): German philosopher; observations on desire and will coincidentally similar to principles of Buddhism.

Joseph Eichendorff (1788–1857): German writer, author of poems set by Schumann.

Percy Bysshe Shelley (1792–1822): English poet; critic of oppressions, organized religion, and convention; *Ozymandias.*

Jean-Baptiste Camille Corot (1796–1875): French painter of realistic landscapes.

Eugene Delacroix (1798–1863): French painter; scenes of war, travels in Africa; *Liberty Leading the People*; portrait of Chopin.

Alexander Pushkin (1799–1837): Russian poet and writer; father of modern Russian literature; operas based on Pushkin include Tchaikovsky's *Eugene Onegin* and *The Queen of Spades.*

Honore Balzac (1799–1850): French author of realistic novels; *Le Pere Goriot, La Cousine Bette.*

Victor Hugo (1802–1885): French poet and writer on political, social, and artistic issues; *Les Miserables, The Hunchback of Notre Dame.*

Alexandre Dumas (1802–1870): French author of adventure novels; *The Three Musketeers, The Count of Monte Cristo.*

Ralph Waldo Emerson (1803–1882): American philosopher, poet, orator, essayist; writings on transcendentalism, abolition of slavery.

John Stuart Mill (1806–1873): English philosopher; *On Liberty.*

Elizabeth Barrett Browning (1806–1861): English poet; *Sonnets from the Portuguese* ("How do I love thee? Let me count the ways").

Henry Wadsworth Longfellow (1807–1882): American poet; *Song of Hiawatha, Paul Revere's Ride.*

Jefferson Davis (1808–1889): leader of Confederacy during U.S. Civil War

Abraham Lincoln (1809–1865): sixteenth president of the United States; *Gettysburg Address, Emancipation Proclamation.*

Edgar Allan Poe (1809–1849): American author; *Fall of the House of Usher, The Raven.*

Alfred Lord Tennyson (1809–1892): English poet; *Idylls of the King, Charge of the Light Brigade.*

Charles Darwin (1809–1882): English naturalist; *On the Origin of the Species, The Descent of Man.*

Robert Browning (1812–1889): English poet; anthologies of poetry and dramatic monologues.

Charles Dickens (1812–1870): Victorian writer of novels on social evils and injustice; *Oliver Twist, Tale of Two Cities, Great Expectations, David Copperfield, Bleak House, A Christmas Carol.*

Soren Kierkegaard (1813–1855): Danish philosopher; writings on social issues and Christian faith.

Otto von Bismarck (1815–1898): German statesman; first chancellor of unified Germany.

Charlotte Bronte (1816–1855): English novelist; *Jane Eyre, Villette.*

Henry David Thoreau (1817–1862): American transcendentalist, naturalist, philosopher; *On the Duty of Civil Disobedience, Walden, The Maine Woods.*

Emily Bronte (1818–1848): English novelist; *Wuthering Heights.*

Karl Marx (1818–1883): German political philosopher and socialist; *Das Kapital.*

Victoria (1819–1901): Queen of England, 1837 to 1901; proclaimed Empress of India, 1877.

George Eliot (1819–1880): pen name of the English novelist Marian Evans; *Adam Bede, Mill on the Floss, Silas Marner, Middlemarch.*

Herman Melville (1819–1891): American novelist; *Moby Dick, Typee, Omoo, Billy Budd.*

Walt Whitman (1819–1892): American poet, journalist, humanist; *Leaves of Grass, Song of Myself.*

Gustave Courbet (1819–1877): French painter of realistic landscapes, seascapes, common people.

John Ruskin (1819–1900): English art and social critic; champion of pre-Raphaelite painters; advocate of conservation and economic socialism.

Gregor Mendel (1822–1884): Austrian monk and geneticist; studies of inherited traits; laws of genetic dominance and recessiveness

Louis Pasteur (1822–1895): French microbiologist; germ theory of disease; developed process of pasteurization; pioneer in fields of vaccination and immunization.

Henrik Ibsen (1828–1906): Norwegian playwright and practitioner of dramatic realism; *Peer Gynt, A Doll's House, Ghosts, An Enemy of the People, The Wild Duck, Hedda Gabler.*

Emily Dickinson (1830–1886): American poet; reflections on nature, love, life, and death distinguished by elusive meanings and idiosyncratic use of rhyme and syntax.

Edouard Manet (1832–1883): French Impressionist painter; scenes of contemporary Parisian life.

Mark Twain (1835–1910): American novelist and humorist; *Adventures of Tom Sawyer, Adventures of Huckleberry Finn, The Prince and the Pauper, A Connecticut Yankee in King Arthur's Court, Life on the Mississippi.*

Winslow Homer (1836–1910): American painter; landscapes and seascapes.

Paul Cezanne (1839–1906): French Impressionist painter; late works anticipate cubism and abstraction in use of natural forms in landscapes, still lifes, portraits.

John D. Rockefeller (1839–1937): American industrialist; founder of Standard Oil.

Claude Monet (1840–1926): French Impressionist painter; explored effects of changing light on color and form; gardens and lily ponds at his home in Giverny.

Pierre Renoir (1840–1919): French Impressionist painter and sculptor; people at leisure, nudes, outdoor scenes.

William James (1842–1910): American philosopher and psychologist; educational psychology; nature of the self, religious belief, conscioness; *Principles of Psychology, The Meaning of Truth.*

Henry James (1843–1916): American writer; *Daisy Miller, Portrait of a Lady, Turn of the Screw.*

Friedrich Nietzsche (1844–1900): German philosopher; *Birth of Tragedy, Thus Spoke Zarathustra.*

Alexander Graham Bell (1847–1922): Scottish-born American inventor in communications; inventor of the telephone and microphone; techniques for teaching speech to the deaf.

Paul Gauguin (1848–1903): French Post-Impressionist painter; richly colored depictions of native life in South Sea islands.

Vincent Van Gogh (1853–1890): Dutch painter; precursor of expressionism; still lifes, self portraits, *Starry Night, Wheatfields with Crows, Bedroom at Arles.*

George Bernard Shaw (1856–1950): English-Irish dramatist, literary and music critic, social activist; 1925 Nobel Prize for Literature; *Pygmalion, Saint Joan, Man and Superman, Heartbreak House.*

Oscar Wilde (1856–1900): Irish poet and playwright; *Picture of Dorian Gray, Lady Windermere's Fan, Importance of Being Earnest, Salome, De Profundis.*

Sigmund Freud (1856–1939): Austrian physician, founder of psychoanalysis; *Interpretation of Dreams.*

John Dewey (1859–1952): American pragmatist philosopher and educator; *Democracy and Education, Art as Experience, Freedom and Culture.*

Arthur Conan Doyle (1859–1930): Scottish author of science fiction, historical novels, crime fiction, creator of Sherlock Holmes.

Edvard Munch (1863-1944): Norwegian painter and printmaker; expressionist themes; *The Scream.*

Henry Ford (1863–1947): American automobile pioneer and manufacturer.

William Butler Yeats (1865–1939): Irish poet and dramatist; 1923 Nobel Prize for Literature; founder of Irish Academy of Letters, published *Oxford Book of Verse.*

CHAPTER 5: EUROPEAN AND AMERICAN ART MUSIC SINCE 1900

As has been true of all periods, music of the last hundred or so years is related to past traditions yet has developed modes of expression that are distinctly modern and depart from earlier practices. Works of art are always in some respect reflective of the time in which they were created and, conversely, shape our perception of the period in which they were produced. Some music readily speaks to us because we are in some way connected to its historical and cultural context, yet often the closer works of art are to us in time, the more alien and inaccessible they seem. This is not a new phenomenon. Artists have traditionally been visionaries, creators of new ways of experiencing and communicating that challenge our comprehension. Insight into the circumstances of a work's genesis and what the composer set out to accomplish can help us listen with more sympathy and understanding.

In the early decades of the 20th century, many creative artists were reacting against the aesthetics and values of Romanticism. The composer Igor Stravinsky and the painter/sculptor Pablo Picasso are among the important figures whose works reflect their interest in tribal societies and the primitive, ritualistic dimension of the human psyche that was the subject of Freud's research and writings. One of the most radical departures from past music traditions was Arnold Schoenberg's "method of composing with twelve tones" that rejected principles of a key center and the distinction between consonance and dissonance that had been the foundation of Western music for centuries. Because of the absence of a tonic, twelve-tone music is often called "atonal," a term to which Schoenberg objected, or "serial" because the compositional technique involves manipulation of a germinal series of pitches. Schoenberg's theoretical writings and his serial works have had great impact on subsequent generations of composers. While twelve-tone describes Schoenberg's compositional procedure, his style is classified as expressionist. Expressionism was an early 20th-century movement that sought to reveal through art the irrational, subconscious reality and repressed primordial impulses postulated and analyzed in the writings of Freud.

Another important development during the early decades of the 20th century was awakening of interest among American visual artists, novelists, poets, playwrights, choreographers, and composers in creating works that reflected a distinctly American, as opposed to a European, sensibility. In music, the renowned Czech composer Antonin Dvorak, who visited the United States during the 1890s, challenged Americans to compose their own music based on native folk materials. His own *Symphony # 9* (1893), written during his stay in America, was evocative of the African American spiritual. By the 1920s American composers like George Gershwin and Aaron Copland were incorporating the rhythms and blues tonality of jazz into their symphonic works. Gershwin's 1924 piece, *Rhapsody in Blue*, is the best-known work from this genre. During the 1930s and early 1940s, Copland, Gershwin, Virgil Thomson, and Roy Harris drew from an array of American folk styles including spirituals, blues, cowboy songs, folk hymns, and fiddle tunes in composing their populist symphonic works.

American composers of the early 20th century also sought to create distinctly new works by engaging in radical experimentation. Charles Ives, writing in the first two decades of the century, was the first American to move away from the Romantic European conventions of form and style by employing dissonance, atonality, complex rhythms, and nonlinear structures. These ideas were continued by the American experimental composers Henry Cowell, Conlon Nancarrow, Edgar Varèse, and Ruth Crawford Seeger in the 1920s and 1930s. By the 1940s and into the post–World War II years, American avant-garde composer John Cage would challenge listeners to completely rethink what constituted music and art through his radically experimental works that drew from new technology, performance art, and Eastern systems of thought and aesthetics. Cage paved the way for the so-called "downtown" New York experimental scene that broke down barriers between music, visual art, performance, and so forth. Cage's interest in non-Western music inspired the minimalist composers including Terry Riley, Steve Reich, and Philip Glass, who would draw on African and Asian musical systems in the 1960s and 1970s.

This interest in non-Western music in the last 50 years is a result of the unprecedented contact between different cultures. For most of human history, musical repertories have evolved largely in isolation from one another, so musical experiences have been principally confined to the music of an individual's own immediate culture. Today the opportunities to hear music and the types of music that are available have expanded dramatically as a result of modern technology and increased contact among peoples. Modern modes of travel and communication and technologies for recording music invented since the end of the 19th century have removed barriers that isolated different musical traditions and repertories from each other. A typical music store in the United States today has sections devoted to recordings covering the entire span of European classical music from the Middle Ages to the present, world music, and repertories that evolved during the 20th century such as jazz and rock. Music from distant times and places is also featured in the programming of some radio stations, television stations, and online music sites. Residents of large cities and those living near college campuses have opportunities to hear live performances by musicians trained in other cultural traditions or specializing in early music, as well as concerts by orchestras, opera companies, and soloists performing standard classical repertory. For musicians, the globalization of music has opened new doors and dissolved old boundaries. Performers study and gain mastery in repertoires of cultures other than their own, and composers can draw on literally the entire world of music in creating new crossover styles.

Modern technology has made possible not only the preservation and broad dissemination of music, but has also become a source for the generation and manipulation of musical sounds. One of the earliest devices that created musical sounds by electronic means, the Theremin (named after its inventor, the Russian scientist, Leon Theremin) was introduced in the early 1920s. Using the numerous technologies that were developed in the following decades, composers recorded musical tones or natural sounds that they transformed by mechanical and electronic means and sometimes supplemented with others generated electronically in a studio. This raw material was then assembled for playback, either as a self-sufficient composition or combined with live performance. Today, technology-based composition has become a widely available process through the storage of sound samples in home computers. Synthesized, sampled, and digitally altered sounds are commonly used for special effects in popular music, movie scores, and works for the concert hall. There is also a repertory in which the tone color dimension of sound is what the work is about. Comparable to the abstract painter whose materials are the basic elements of shape and color, the composer constructs a succession of aural events of unique tone color, dynamics, and registration.

Historic Context

Marconi transmits telegraphic radio messages, 1901.

Henry Ford founds Ford Motor Company, 1903.

Wright brothers' first airplane flight, 1903.

First Tour de France bicycle race, 1903.

First World Series in baseball, 1904.

Broadway subway opens, 1904.

First cubist exhibition in Paris, 1907.

W. E. B. DuBois founds NAACP, 1910.

Manhattan Bridge is completed, 1910.

S.S. Titanic sinks on maiden voyage, 1912.

Sixteenth Amendment to the U.S. Constitution introduces federal income tax, 1913.

Grand Central Terminal opens, 1913.

Niels Bohr formulates theory of atomic structure, 1913.

Panama Canal opens, 1914.

World War I, 1914–1918.

Eighteenth Amendment to the U.S. Constitution prohibits manufacture, sale, or importation of alcoholic beverages, 1920; repealed 1933.

Founding of the League of Nations, 1920; U.S. Senate votes against joining.

Nineteenth Amendment to the U.S. Constitution gives women the right to vote.

Soviet states form USSR, 1922.

Scopes trial in Tennessee on teaching of theory of evolution, 1925.

Charles Lindbergh solo flight across the Atlantic, 1927.

Museum of Modern Art opens in New York City, 1929.

Stock market crash, beginning of world economic crisis, 1929.

Building of the Empire State Building, 1929–1931.

George Washington Bridge is completed, 1931.

United States enters World War II, 1940.

Enrico Fermi splits the atom, 1942.

First atomic bomb detonated, New Mexico, 1945.

United States drops atomic bombs on Hiroshima and Nagasaki, Japan, 1945; Japan surrenders.

Nuremberg trials of Nazi war criminals begin, 1945.

Jackie Robinson becomes first African American major league baseball player, 1947.

Founding of the State of Israel, 1948.

United Nations building in New York City is completed, 1950.

United States explodes first hydrogen bomb at Pacific atoll, 1952.

U.S.S.R. explodes hydrogen bomb, 1953.

U.S.S.R. launches Sputnik I and II, first earth satellites, 1957.

Guggenheim Museum opens, 1958.

Berlin wall is constructed, 1961.

Assassination of President John Fitzgerald Kennedy, 1963.

Martin Luther King, Jr. wins Noble Peace Prize, 1964; assassinated, 1968.

Apollo landing and moon walk, 1969.

Paris Peace Accords to end Vietnam War, 1973.

Three Mile Island nuclear accident, 1979.

Sandra Day O'Connor appointed first female justice of U.S. Supreme Court, 1981.

Vietnam Veterans' War Memorial dedicated in Washington, DC, 1982.

AIDS virus discovered by U.S. and French research teams, 1984.

Bishop Desmond Tutu of South African Council of Churches receives Nobel Peace Prize, 1984.

Chernobyl nuclear accident, 1986.

Challenger disaster, 1986.

Soviet invasion of Afghanistan, 1988.

Pan Am 103 is blown up over Lockerbie, Scotland, 1988.

Exxon Valdez oil spill in Alaska, 1989.

Tianemen Square massacre, 1989.

Solidarity wins first free election in Poland since World War II, 1989.
Fall of the Berlin Wall, 1989.
Reunification of Germany, 1990.
Mikhail Gorbachev elected first president of the Soviet Union; awarded Nobel Peace Prize, 1990.
Hubble Space Telescope put into orbit, 1990.
Iraq invades Kuwait, 1990.
Operation Desert Storm; end of the Gulf War, 1991.
Warsaw Pact dissolved, 1991.
Collapse of the Soviet Union, 1991.
World Trade Center bombing in parking garage, 1993.
Nelson Mandela inaugurated as South Africa's first president, 1994.
Successful cloning of Dolly the sheep, 1996.
Terrorist attacks on World Trade Center, the Pentagon, crash of United flight 175, 2001.
U.S. administration declares War on Terrorism, 2001.
United States attacks Afghanistan, 2002.
Introduction of the Euro currency, 2002.
Space shuttle Columbia disintegrates on reentry, 2003.
Iraq war begins; Bush declares end of fighting, 2003.

Milestones in Music

First phonograph recording by opera great Enrico Caruso, 1902.
Manhattan Opera House built in New York, 1903.
First recording of an opera, Verdi's *Ernani*, 1903.
First radio transmission of music, 1904.
Lev Theremin invents earliest electronic musical instrument, 1927.
First annual Newport Jazz Festival, 1954.
Stereophonic recordings introduced, 1958.
Opening of the Rock & Roll Hall of Fame, Cleveland, Ohio, 1995.

Major Figures in Music

Arnold Schoenberg (1874–1951): Austrian-born composer; see Musician Biographies.
Charles Ives (1874–1954): American composer; see Musician Biographies.
Bela Bartok (1881–1945): Hungarian composer; see Musician Biographies.
Edgard Varèse (1883–1965): French avant-garde composer; see Musician Biographies.
Sergei Prokofiev (1891–1953): Soviet composer.
Bessie Smith (1894–1937): American blues singer; see Musician Biographies.
George Gershwin (1898–1937): American composer; see Musician Biographies.
Lillian Hardin (1898–1971): American pianist and composer; see Musician Biographies.
Paul Robeson (1898–1976): American singer, actor, political activist.
Edward Kennedy "Duke" Ellington (1899–1974): American jazz composer and bandleader; see Musician Biographies.
Aaron Copland (1900–1990): American composer; see Musician Biographies.
Louis Armstrong (1901–1971): American jazz composer and performer; see Musician Biographies.
Ruth Crawford Seeger (1901–1953): composer and folk music transcriber; see Musician Biographies.
Earl Hines (1905–1983): American jazz pianist and composer.
Dmitry Shostakovich (1906–1975): Soviet composer.
Benny Goodman (1909–1986): American clarinetist and jazz bandleader.
Woody Guthrie (1912–1967): American folk singer.
Mahalia Jackson (1912–1972): American gospel singer.
Billie Holiday (1915–1959): American blues singer.
Thelonious Monk (1917–1982): American jazz pianist and composer; see Musician Biographies.

Dizzy Gillespie (1917–1993): American trumpeter.

Leonard Bernstein (1918–1990): American composer and conductor; see Musician Biographies.

Pete Seeger (b. 1919): New York City urban folk singer; see Musician Biographies.

Charlie Parker (1920–1955): American jazz musician; see Musician Biographies.

Charles Mingus (1923–1979): American jazz bassist and composer.

Ravi Shankar (b. 1920): Indian sitar virtuoso and composer; see Musician Biographies.

Bill Haley (1925–1981): American rock bandleader and composer.

BB King (b. 1925): influential blues musician; see Musician Biographies.

John Coltrane (1926–1967): jazz saxophonist; see Musician Biographies.

Miles Davis (1926–1991): American jazz musician; see Musician Biographies.

Miles Davis (1926–1991): American jazz trumpeter, composer, bandleader.

Stephen Sondheim (b. 1930): American musical theater composer.

Elvis Presley (1935–1977): American rock-and-roll singer; see Musician Biographies.

Steve Reich (b. 1936): American minimalist composer; see Musician Biographies.

John Lennon (1940–1980): English pop musician and composer.

Frank Zappa (1940–1993): American rock musician, bandleader, composer.

Bob Dylan (b. 1941): American folk singer; see Musician Biographies.

Bob Marley (1945–1981): Jamaican reggae musician.

Michael Jackson (b. 1958): American rock singer and songwriter.

Other Historic Figures

Sigmund Freud (1856–1939): Austrian neurologist, founder of psychoanalysis.

Joseph Conrad (1857–1924): English novelist.

Alfred North Whitehead (1861–1947): English mathematician and philosopher.

Edvard Munch (1863–1944): Norwegian painter.

Alfred Stieglitz (1864–1946): American photographer.

Frank Lloyd Wright (1869–1959): American architect.

Mahatma Gandhi (1869–1948): Indian nationalist and pacifist.

Orville Wright (1871–1948): American aircraft pioneer.

Bertrand Russell (1872–1970): British philosopher.

Willa Cather (1873–1947): American novelist and short story writer.

Winston Churchill (1874–1965): British statesman.

Robert Frost (1874–1963): American poet.

Thomas Mann (1875–1955): German novelist; Nobel Prize 1929.

D. W. Griffith (1875–1948): American director of 484 films.

Jack London (1876–1916): American novelist.

Hermann Hesse (1877–1946): German author; Nobel Prize 1946.

Martin Buber (1878–1965): Austrian Jewish philosopher.

Carl Sandburg (1878–1967): American poet.

Albert Einstein (1879–1955): German physicist; Nobel Prize, 1921.

Pablo Picasso (1881–1973): Spanish-born artist, active chiefly in France.

James Joyce (1882–1941): Irish novelist.

Virginia Woolf (1882–1941): English novelist and critic.

Edward Hopper (1882–1967): American painter.

Benito Mussolini (1883–1945): Italian fascist dictator.

Franz Kafka (1883–1924): German writer.

D. H. Lawrence (1885–1930): English novelist.

Edna St. Vincent Millet (1892–1950): American poet.

Sinclair Lewis (1895–1951): American novelist, Noble Prize, 1930.

Oskar Kokoschka (1886–1980): Austrian Expressionist painter.

Diego Rivera (1886–1957): Mexican painter and muralist.

Le Corbusier (1887–1965): French architect.

Georgia O'Keefe (1887–1986): American painter.

Marc Chagall (1887–1985): Russian-born French painter.

T. S. Eliot (1888–1965): American poet.
Eugene O'Neill (1888–1953): American playwright.
Adolf Hitler (1889–1945): Nazi dictator.
Martha Graham (1893–1991): American dancer, choreographer, teacher, director.
Mao Tse-tung (1893–1976): founder of Chinese Communist Party, leader People's Republic of China.
F. Scott Fitzgerald (1896–1940): American novelist.
Ernest Hemingway (1899–1961): American novelist; Pulitzer Prize, 1952.
Martin Heidegger (1889–1969): German philosopher.
Vladimir Nabakov (1899–1977): Russian-born American novelist.
Alfred Hitchcock (1899–1980): English-born American film director.
Enrico Fermi (1901–1954): Italian physicist; Nobel Prize, 1938.
John Steinbeck (1902–1968): American novelist; Pulitzer Prize, 1940.
George Orwell (1903–1950): English author.
Graham Greene (1904–1991): English novelist.
Salvador Dali (1904–1989): Spanish painter.
J. Robert Oppenheimer (1904–1967): American nuclear physicist.
B. F. Skinner (1904–1990): American psychologist.
Jean-Paul Sartre (1905–1980): French author and philosopher.
Samuel Becket (1906–1989): Irish dramatist.
Frida Kahlo (1907–1954): Mexican painter.
Jackson Pollock (1912–1956): American painter.
Albert Camus (1913–1960): French author.
Ralph Ellison (1914–1994): American novelist.
Saul Bellow (b. 1915): American novelist.
Arthur Miller (b. 1915): American playwright.
Norman Mailer (b. 1923): American novelist.
Allen Ginsberg (1926–1997): American poet and political activist.
Andy Warhol (1928–1987): American artist and filmmaker.
Gabriel Garcia Marquez (b. 1928): Colombian novelist; Nobel Prize for Literature, 1982.
Martin Luther King, Jr. (1929–1968): American civil rights leader; Nobel Peace Prize, 1964.
Toni Morrison (b. 1931): American novelist.

CHAPTER 6: AMERICAN VERNACULAR MUSIC

Introduction

Western culture has tended to divide musical practices into two very broad fields, the vernacular and the cultivated. Vernacular refers to everyday, informal musical practices located outside the official arena of high culture—the conservatory, the concert hall, and the high church. The field of vernacular music is often further subdivided into the domains of folk music (orally transmitted and community based) and popular music (mediated for a mass audience). Cultivated music, often referred to as classical or art music, is associated with formal training and written composition. The boundaries between so-called folk, popular, and classical music are becoming increasingly blurred as we enter into the 21st century, due to the pervasive effects of mass media that have made music of all American ethnic/racial groups, classes, and regions available to everyone.

Historians and musicologists now agree that America's most distinctive musical expressions are found, or have roots in, its vernacular music. Early immigrants from Western Europe and the slaves stolen from Africa brought with them rich traditions of oral folk music that mixed and mingled throughout the 18th and 19th centuries to develop uniquely American ballads, instrumental dance music, and spirituals. By the early 20th century, the folk blues emerged and would go on to form the foundation of much of our popular music. Beginning with 19th century minstrel and parlor song collections, and threading through the 20th century recordings of Tin Pan Alley song, gospel, rhythm and blues, country, rock, soul, and rap, the print and electronic media fueled the growth of American popular musical styles that today have proliferated across the globe. Jazz, sometimes considered America's "classical" music, certainly had roots in early 20th century folk and popular styles (see Chapter 7: Jazz). And many of America's best-known classical composers including George Gershwin, Aaron Copland, Virgil Thomson, and Duke Ellington based their extended compositions on vernacular folk and popular themes (see Chapter 5: European and American Art Music since 1900).

American Folk Music

Folk music was once thought of as being simple, old, anonymously composed music played by poor, rural, nonliterate people representing the lower strata of our society (mountain hillbillies, southern black sharecroppers, cowboys, etc.). Today scholars have expanded the field by defining folk music as orally transmitted songs and instrumental expressions that are passed on in community settings and generally show a degree of stability over time. Rather than viewing folk expressions as vanishing antiquities, this perspective suggests folk music can be a dynamic process that continues to flourish within many communities of our modern society. Using this model popular music may be defined as mass-mediated expression that changes rapidly over time, and classical/art music as musical practices centered in formal training and written composition.

In the late 19th and early 20th centuries, American folk music collectors wrote down the words and melodies to a variety of traditional expressions including Native American ritual songs, African American spirituals and work songs, Anglo American ballads and fiddle tunes, and western cowboy songs. Later they broadened their interest to include the traditional expressions of ethnic and immigrant communities such as the practices of Hispanic, Irish, Jewish, Caribbean, and Chinese Americans, most of whom lived in urban areas. With the advent of portable recording technology in the 1930s, folklorists like Alan Lomax began the task of documenting America's folk music and compiling the Archive of American Folk Song, which today, along with the Smithsonian Folkways Recordings, offers students the chance to hear and study authentic regional folk styles.

Most Anglo and African American folk genres are built around relatively simple (often pentatonic) melodies, duple or triple meter time signatures, and a series of harmonic structures built around the tonic, subdominant, and dominant chords. But much of the emotional appeal of folk music comes from the grain or tension of the voice. Vocal textures vary greatly, ranging from the high, tense, nasal delivery associated with white mountain singers, to the more relaxed, throaty, rough timbre of southern African American blues and spiritual singers.

In addition to studying song texts and melodies, folk music scholars have paid a great deal of attention to the social function of folk music. They seek to understand how a particular song or instrumental piece works within a specific social situation for a particular group of people. For example, how do Native American chants and African American spirituals operate within the context of a religious or worship ceremony; how are Anglo and Celtic American fiddle tunes central to Appalachian and community gatherings; how did traditional blues and ballads reflect contrasting world views of southern blacks and whites; and how do West Indian steel bands and Jewish klezmer ensembles serve as markers of cultural pride?

The self-conscious revival of folk music by middle-class urban Americans has been going on since the 1930s. During the Depression and WWII years, folk artists like Louisiana-born Huddie "Lead Belly" Ledbetter and Oklahoma-born Woody Guthrie introduced city audiences to rural folk music, and along with left-leaning topical folk singers like Pete Seeger, they helped spawn the great folk revival of the post–World War II years. Folk music spilled into the popular arena with artists like the Kingston Trio; Burl Ives; Peter, Paul & Mary; and Bob Dylan writing and recording hit folk songs.

Anglo American Ballads

Ballads are basically folk songs that tell stories through the introduction of characters in a specific situation, the building up of dramatic tension, and the resolution of that tension. Ballads were originally brought to America by British, Scottish, and Scotch-Irish immigrants, many of whom eventually settled in the mountainous regions of the American south.

The melodies of Anglo American ballads are simple, often built around archaic sounding pentatonic (five note) and hexatonic (six-tone) scales that may feature large jumps or gaps between notes. Songs are traditionally sung a cappella in a free meter style, or with simple guitar or banjo accompaniment. The voice is delivered in a high, tense, nasal style.

Ballads are most often set in four line stanzas, with the second and fourth line rhyming:

> I was born in West Virginia,
>   among the beautiful hills.
> And the memory of my childhood,
>   lies deep within me still.

While older British and Scottish ballads found in the American South dealt with themes of ancient kings, queens, and magical happenings in faraway places, the 18th- and 19th -century ballads that developed in America tell stories of everyday folk involved in everyday life events, usually set in the present or recent past. Sentimental and tragic love stories, often involving violence and death, were common. Many American ballads express strong moral sentiments, warning listeners about the consequences of irresponsible behavior:

> I courted a fair maiden,
> her name I will not tell
> For I have now disgraced her,
> and I am doomed to hell.
>
> It was on one beautiful evening,
> the stars were shining bright
> And with that faithful dagger,
> I did her spirit flight.
>
> So justice overtook me,
> you all can plainly see.
> My soul is doomed forever,
> throughout eternity.

The sentimental and tragic themes of Anglo American ballads, along with the high-pitched, "whiny" vocal style, have survived and flourished in 20th-century popular country music.

African American Spirituals and Gospel Music

The African American Spiritual has its origins in the religious practices of 18th- and 19th -century American slaves who converted to Christianity during the great awakening revivals. The earliest spirituals were African-style ring shouts, based on simple call and response lyrics chanted against a driving rhythm produced by clapping and foot stomping. Participants would shuffle around in a ring-formation and "shout" when they felt the spirit. More complex melodies and verse/chorus structures began to evolve, reflecting the influence of European American hymn singing, and accompaniment by guitar, piano, and percussion became common. Vocal ornamentations (slides, glides, extended use of falsetto), call and response singing, and blues tonality characterized these folk spirituals. In the reconstruction period black college choirs such as the Fisk Jubilee Singers arranged folk spirituals into four-part harmony, a form that became known as the concert spiritual. A blend of African and European musical practices, the spiritual epitomizes the sycretic (blended) nature of much American folk music resulting from the mixing of Africans and Europeans in the Americas.

The texts of many spirituals are taken from Old Testament themes and stories. The slaves were particularly moved by Old Testament figures like Daniel (who was saved from the lion's den), Jonah (who was delivered from the belly of the whale), Noah (who survived the flood), and David (who defeated the giant Goliath) who struggled and triumphed over adverse conditions. The plight of the Israelites and their escape from bondage to the promised land was an especially powerful story retold by the spirituals:

When Israel was in Egypt's land,
    O let my people go!
Oppressed so hard they could not stand,
    O let my people go!

Go Down, Moses,
Away down to Egypt's land.
And tell old Pharaoh,
To let my people go!

The spiritual's emphasis on redemption and deliverance in this world have led historians to suggest the songs had double meaning for the slaves—they affirmed their belief in the Bible as well as their trust that a just God would deliver them from the evils of slavery. The spirituals are thus seen as expressions of religious faith and resistance to slavery.

In the 20th-century spirituals evolved into the more urban, New Testament–centered gospel songs. Following the first "great migration" of southern African Americans to urban centers like Chicago, New York, and Philadelphia in the post–Word War I years, a new genre of black American sacred songs known as gospel began to appear. Unlike the anonymous folk spirituals, gospel songs were composed and copyrighted by songwriters like Thomas Dorsey and Reverend William Herbert Brewster, and by the 1930s were being recorded by urban church singers. Some, like Mahalia Jackson, the Dixie Hummingbirds, and the Ward Singers, turned professional and reached national and international audiences through their tours and recordings. But most gospel singing remained rooted in African American church ritual, and to this day can be heard in black communities throughout the north and south.

Musically, gospel is a blending of spirituals, blues, and the song sermons of the black preacher. Gospel songs are usually organized in a 16- or 32-bar verse/chorus form, often featuring call-and-response singing between a leader and a chorus. Blues tonalities are common, and singers are known for their intensive vocal ornamentations, which include bending and slurring notes, falsetto swoops, and melismas (groups of notes or tones sung across one syllable of a word). Gospel singers often end a song with a prolonged section of improvisation that combines singing, chanting, and shouting in hopes of "bringing down the spirit." Lyrics are most often New Testament–centered, focusing on the redeeming power of Jesus and the singer's personal relationship with the Savior.

Although gospel lyrics are strictly religious in nature, gospel music derives much of its sound from blues and jazz. Likewise, gospel music has been a source for various secular styles, including early rock and roll, soul music, and most recently gospel rap. During the Civil Rights era the melodies of old spirituals and gospel songs were used with new lyrics expressing the need to overcome Jim Crow segregation.

The Blues

Blues music was the first significant form of secular music created by African American ex-slaves in the deep South in the late 19th and early 20th centuries. Growing out of earlier black spirituals, work songs, field hollers, and dance music, the blues addressed the social experiences of the ex-slaves as they struggled to establish themselves in post–Reconstruction southern culture.

Common themes addressed in early country blues songs were conflicts in love relations, loneliness, hardship, poverty, and travel. But it would be a mistake to assume that the blues were exclusively about sorrow—blues celebrated life's ups and downs, and often reflected a keen sense of ironic wit and a resolve to struggle on against difficult circumstances.

Most of the early recordings of country blues from the 1920s feature a solo male singer like Charlie Patton, Blind Lemon Jefferson, Blind Blake, and Son House, accompanying himself with an acoustic guitar. But blues singers also used banjos, mandolins, fiddles, and harmonicas, and often played in small ensembles that provided dance music at country juke joints. Although blues has been interpreted as a highly individualistic expression because of the solo voice and first person text, the music was often played in social settings where African Americans danced, communed, and solidified their group identity.

Early blues lyrics were built around rhymed couplets that eventually became standardized in a 12-bar (measure) format that featured an AAB structure, with a couplet being repeated twice, and answered by a second couplet:

> I woke up this morning,
>> I was feeling sad and blue. [A]
> I woke up the morning,
>> I was feeling sad and blue. [A]
> My sweet gal she left me,
>> got no one to sing my troubles to. [B]

The tonality is major, most often built around a 12-bar (measure) progression of the I (tonic), IV (subdominant), and V (dominant) chords. The melodic line often features bent and slurred notes, with generous use of the flatted third and seventh tones (known as "blue" notes) of the diatonic scale. The meter is usually duple (4/4), and tempos may vary from a slow drag to a fast boogie.

While the first blues were undoubtedly rural in origin, by the 1920s blues music had made its way to the city. Urban singers like Ma Rainey and Bessie Smith recorded and popularized sophisticated, jazz-tinged arrangements of blues in the 1920s, and composers like W. C. Handy incorporated blues forms into popular orchestral pieces like "St. Louis Blues" and "Memphis Blues." In the post–World War II years the country blues was electrified and transformed into rhythm and blues (R&B) by Chicago-based artists Muddy Waters (McKinley Morganfield), Howlin' Wolf (Chester Burnett), and Elmore James, and Memphis bluesman B. B. King. By the mid-1950s southern white singers like Elvis Presley, Jerry Lee Lewis, and Buddy Holly were blending rhythm and blues with elements of country music to create the new pop genre of rock and roll.

Rock and Roll

Perhaps America's most influential contribution to the world of popular music has been the development of rock and roll in the 1950s. Many streams of folk and vernacular music styles, including blues, spirituals, gospel, ballads, hillbilly music, and early jazz, contributed to the evolution of rock and roll (R&R). But it was the convergence of African American rhythm and blues and Anglo American honky-tonk (country) music that led to the emergence of a distinctive new style that would dominate the field of popular music in post–World War II America.

Honky-tonk, often referred to as the voice of the downcast, working-class southern whites, was the dominant form of country music during the 1940s and early 1950s, with Hank Williams being its most famous practitioner. The music featured the tense, nasal vocal style associated with the earlier ballad tradition, accompanied by twangy guitars and fiddles, and lyrics centered on stories of loneliness and broken love relationships. Rhythm and blues was an urbanized version of older country blues that developed in cities like Memphis and Chicago during and immediately after the Second World War. Singers like Muddy Waters, Howlin' Wolf, and B. B. King shouted and pleaded to their audiences, backed by screaming electric guitars, amplified harmonicas, and a rhythm sections of drums, bass, and piano. The music was loud, aggressive, and sensual, with lyrics boasting of sexual conquest or lamenting failed love.

The earliest rock-and-roll recordings were made by both white and black singers in the mid-1950s. The southern white artists like Elvis Presley, Johnny Cash, Carl Perkins, Jerry Lee Lewis, and Bill Haley were dubbed rockabillies because their sounds were rooted in hillbilly and honky-tonk country styles. Their covers of black rhythm and blues songs like "Rock Around the Clock" (Haley) and "Good Rockin' Tonight" (Presley) provided some of the first and most powerful examples of how white country and black R&B could blend to form the new style of R&R. From the other side of the racial divide came black R&B singers like Chuck Berry, Little Richard, and Fats Domino, who cut their R&B sound with smoother vocals (and in Berry's case country-influenced guitar licks) to forge a black style of R&R that was close (and at times indistinguishable) from that of their white counterparts.

Thus, R&R was the inevitable result of an interracial musical stew that had been simmering in the southern United States for several centuries. Its appearance in the mid-1950s was no accident, because this was precisely when independent record companies like Sun (Memphis) and Chess (Chicago) and innovative radio stations like WDIA (Memphis) were beginning to bring black vernacular music to a burgeoning baby boomer audience and the nascent civil rights movements was increasing public awareness of black culture. R&R was a popular style created in the studio and marketed directly for legions of young, predominantly white consumers who, thanks to the relative affluence of the post–World War II years, were in search of new leisure activities.

Musically the earliest R&R recordings were 12-bar blues played in an up-tempo 4/4 meter. Singers, black and white, would sometimes shout and snarl, but were careful to articulate their words in a style smooth enough for their predominantly white audiences to comprehend. The music was backed by a strong, insistent rhythm that accented the second and fourth beat of each measure, creating a sound that was easy to dance to. Rock's gyrating singers and sensual dancing led many middle-class Americans, black and white, to condemn it as an immoral and corrupting force. When Elvis Presley first appeared on the nationally broadcast TV variety show hosted by Ed Sullivan in 1956, the cameras would only show him from the waist up in order to avoid his sexy moves that had earned him the title "Elvis the Pelvis."

The lyrics to the most successful early R&R songs centered on teenage romance and adventure, recounting high times cruising in automobiles, dancing at the hop, and falling in and out of love. The lyrics to sexually suggestive R&B songs covered by R&R singers were consciously cleaned up so the music would be less offensive to middle-class (black and white) teens and their parents. Eventually the 12-bar blues form was eclipsed by the verse/chorus structure organized in 8- or 16-bar stanzas. As in earlier American popular songs, the repeated chorus was usually based on a simple but engaging melody (often referred to as the "hook") that was easy to sing along to.

In the 1960s groups like the Beatles and folk rock singer Bob Dylan transformed R&R by writing more sophisticated lyrics addressing the complexities of love and sexual relations, alienation in Western society, and the utopian search for a new world through drugs and counterculture activities. Both American and British rock groups of the 1960s demonstrated that popular music could provide serious social commentary that had previously been associated with the arenas of modern art and literature and the urban folksong movement. Over the past four decades R&R (often referred to as "rock" to differentiate it from the R&R of the 1950s) has evolved in many directions (art rock, heavy metal, punk, indie), often cross-pollinating with related styles like soul, funk, disco, country, reggae, and most recently hip-hop. At times rock has served as the political voice of angry and alienated youth, and at other times simply as good-time party and dance music.

Rap

Rap is poetry recited rhythmically over musical accompaniment. Rap is part of hip-hop culture, which emerged in the mid-1970s in the Bronx. Graffiti art and break-dance are the other major elements of hip-hop culture. Rap lyrics display clever use of words and rhymes, verbal dexterity, and intricate rhythmic patterning. Rap artists take on different roles and speak from perspectives ranging from comedic to political to dramatic, often narrating stories that reflect or comment on contemporary urban life. Rap artists may be soloists, or members of a rap group (or crew), and may recite in call-and-response format. Rap songs are generally in duple meter at a medium tempo (about 80 to 90 bpm). The musical accompaniment of rap is made up of one or several continuously repeated short phrases, each phrase combining relatively simple rhythmic patterns produced by acoustic and/or synthetic percussion instruments. Other sounds are often added for timbral variety, textural complexity, and melodic/harmonic interest. A bass line provided by electric bass guitar or synthesizer reinforces the meter and defines the tonal center.

Old School Rap (1974-1986)

Old school rap was created by DJs (disc jockeys) and one or more MCs (originally Master of Ceremonies, later Microphone Controller). DJ Kool Herc began this period, providing a portable sound system and spinning records for dances at outdoor parties and small social clubs. He noticed that b-boys and b-girls favored dancing to the "break" in a record, the short section of a song when the band drops out and the percussion continues. Using two copies of the same record on two turntables, Herc was able to make the break repeat continuously, creating the "breakbeat" that became the basic musical structure over which the MC spoke or rapped. DJs Grandmaster Flash, Jazzy Jeff, and Grand Wizard Theodore invented additional turntable techniques: "blending" different records together, scratching (manually moving the record back and forth on the turntable to create rhythmic patterns with scratchy timbres), and mixing in synthetic drum sounds and other effects. An excellent example of turntable techniques is Flash's *The Adventures of Grandmaster Flash on the Wheels of Steel* (1981). DJs, most importantly Afrika Bambaataa, also promoted hip-hop culture through parties and other events spread by word of mouth and at venues throughout New York City.

At first MCs spoke over records in the Jamaican DJ traditions of toasting (calling out friends' names) and boasting (touting the superiority of their own sound system and DJ skills). Both traditions became central elements of the assertive and competitive spirit of rap and hip-hop. Rap drew on other African-American sources for some of its important features: the improvisational verbal skills and call-and-response format of *the dozens* (an African-American verbal competition trading witty insults), the rhyming aphorisms of heavyweight champion Mohammed Ali ("Float like a butterfly, sting like a bee / Your hands can't hit what your eyes can't see"), the songs and vocal stylings of the great soul-funk artist James Brown, and The Last Poets, whose members spoke or chanted politically charged poems over drumming.

The first MCs to develop extended lyrical forms by rhyming over break beats were Grandmaster Caz and DJ Hollywood. The interplay of vocal and accompaniment rhythms, rhyme schemes, and phrasing are the main elements of what is known as flow. Old school flow is more regular and less syncopated than later styles. Two-line units (couplets) rhyming at the end of the lines are common during this period, such as, "Pump it up homeboy, just don't stop / Chef Boy-ar-dee coolin' on the pot" (The Beastie Boys). Before rap entered into the mainstream entertainment industry, portable cassette players provided a cheap and robust route of dissemination for the music throughout the city. It was the success of Sugar Hill Gang's *Rapper's Delight*, issued on a small independent label in 1979, that brought rap to national attention and gave the genre its name. MC Kurtis Blow's *The Breaks* (1980), and *Rapture* by the pop group Blondie (1981) are also milestones in the early history of rap.

During the first part of the 1980's the entertainment industry was slow to realize rap's potential and it was left to entrepreneurs like Russell Simmons to popularize rap and to demonstrate its long-term commercial viability by organizing national hip-hop concert tours and producing hits by many of the most important artists of the period including L.L. Cool J, Slick Rick, and Foxy Brown. Independent films like *Wild Style*, *Beat Street*, and *Style Wars*, introduced hip-hop to a global audience. Rap music videos began to be produced and all-rap radio stations began broadcasting. Independent labels gained ground and rap was incorporated into the established recording and distribution industry. By 1986 hip-hop culture was the most successful popular music in the nation, and rap had developed in three general directions. *Pop rap* (or *party rap*) is light, danceable, and often humorous; it quickly became a crossover genre, generating national hits by Salt-N-Pepa (the first successful female rap group), MC Hammer, Vanilla Ice, and many others. *Rock rap* combines the vocalizations of rap with the sounds and rhythms of rock bands. The hip-hop trio Run-D.M.C. brought rap rock to national prominence with *King of Rock* (the first hip-hop platinum album, 1985). The Beastie Boys, the first white rap group, appealed to a youth market by smartly combining humor and rebellion in songs from their 1986 debut album *Licensed to Ill*. Rock rap set the stage for other hybrids that flourished in the 1990's such as Rage Against the Machine and Linkin Park. *Socially conscious rap* portrays and comments on the urban ills of poverty, crime, drugs, and racism. The first example is Melle Mel's *The Message* (1982), a series of bleak pictures of life and death in the ghetto.

New School Rap

New school rap dates from 1986 when Rakim and DJ Eric B introduced a vocal style that was faster and rhythmically more complex than the simple sing-song couplets of much old school rap. Writers (rap poets/performers) in the new "effusive" style, notably Nas, employed irregular poetic meters, asymmetric phrasing, and intricate rhyme schemes, all of which added depth and complexity to the flow. Much of the new music (and new styles of graffiti and dance) came from the West Coast, and increasingly from the South and Midwest. Hip-hop culture was spreading to Europe and Asia as well.

The accompaniment for rap also became more complex and varied. CD's largely replaced vinyl records and samplers became commercially available. Producers working with samplers, programmable drum machines, and synthesizers could, with the push of a button, mix and modify sounds imported from a virtually unlimited selection, and so largely replaced DJs as the creators of rap's musical accompaniment. The New York production team Bomb Squad and producers RZA and DJ Premier layered multiple samples to create dense, harmonically rich textures and grating "out of tune" combinations of sounds, while West Coast producers developed G-funk by using live instrumentation and conventional harmonies associated with funk music.

The year 1988 was an important turning point for rap. The Source, the first magazine devoted to rap and hip-hop, appeared that year, and was soon followed by Vibe, XXL and many others. The first nationally televised rap music videos on Fab Five Freddy's weekly show "Yo, MTV Raps!" brought hip-hop images and dances to national attention. That same year four new rap genres emerged, partly in response to worsened social conditions in black urban communities: unemployment, drastic cutbacks in education, the crack cocaine epidemic, proliferation of deadly weapons, gang violence, militaristic police tactics, and Draconian drug laws all leading to an explosion in the prison population. *Political rap* was led by writer KRS-One, with Boogie Down Productions whose album *By All Means Necessary* explored police corruption, violence in the hip-hop community, and other controversial topics. On the West Coast, N.W.A. were cultivating harsh timbres and a raw angry sound in their nihilistic tales of Los Angeles police violence and gang life in *Straight Outta Compton*, the first *gangsta rap* album. *Jazz rap*, characterized by use of samples from jazz classics and positive, uplifting lyrics was introduced by Gang Starr (DJ Premier and MC Guru) and hip-hop group Stetsasonic. Another answer to West Coast gangsta rap was New York *hardcore rap*, led by producer Marley Marl whose hip-hop collective The Juicy Crew achieved their breakthrough with the posse track *The Symphony*. Each genre had important followers. Black nationalism informed the political lyrics of Public Enemy (led by Chuck D) whose critical and commercial success in 1988-90 proved the crossover appeal of the new wave of socially conscious rap. Houston-based gangsta rap group The Geto Boys combined ultra-violent fantasies with cutting social commentary in a blues-inflected style that came to characterize the "Dirty South" sound in their 1990 debut album. Jazz rap's Afrocentric lyrics, fashion, and imagery were shared by important new rap artists Queen Latifah and Busta Rhymes. Latifah provided a feminist response to the often misogynist lyrics of male rappers. Wu-Tang Clan's *Enter the Wu-Tang* (1993) reclaimed New York's reputation for cutting-edge hardcore rap. The minimalist production style on the album by this Staten Island group was much imitated through the next decade.

In the 1990's a style called *new jack swing* originating with producers Teddy Riley and Puff Daddy integrated R&B into rap and softened rap's hardcore content while retaining the edge of black street culture. Notorious B.I.G.'s *Juicy* from *Ready to Die* (1994) exemplifies the laid-back vocal delivery and slower tempo that characterize new jack. Lil' Kim's rap on *Gettin' Money* captures the "ghettofabulous" image of the new jack rapper in lyrics that mix gats and six-shooters with Armani and Chanel. The song draws on the iconic American figure of the Mafia don to create metaphors that celebrate materialism and luxury. Tupac Shakur and Notorious B.I.G. were the most critically acclaimed and best-selling rappers during the middle of the 1990's. Shakur was murdered in 1996 and Notorious B.I.G. in 1997. In the eyes of many fans, hip-hop had lost its two greatest artists. Three important figures—Eminem, Jay-Z, and Missy Elliott—led rap into the new millennium.

– Marc Thorman

CHAPTER 7: JAZZ

Characteristic Features

Although most people have heard of jazz, and many recognize it when they hear it, the music is notoriously hard to categorize. There is simply no single description that can account for the vast number of styles and genres that have been placed under the jazz "umbrella." In fact, some musicians (Duke Ellington, Randy Weston, and others) have avoided using the term altogether, finding the concept too confining. The term itself (and its variant "jass") did not appear until the 1910s, after jazz was already a well-established idiom, and has been applied to many types of music that most purists would not consider "true" jazz at all, from the novelty piano rags of Zez Confrey in the 1920s to the instrumental pop music of Kenny G in the 1980s and 1990s.

A few general comments can be made about the music, however. We know, first of all, that jazz was a music created primarily by African Americans, and it has deep roots in traditions that go back as far as the African traditions brought by slaves to America during the Middle Passage. Related to this are two dualities that virtually all types of jazz share. These dualities create a vibrant tension in the music that gives jazz much of its power.

Spontaneity vs. planning
Contrary to some popular beliefs, playing jazz is not simply a matter of musicians playing whatever they feel like. Improvisation—creating new music on the spot—is a vital part of almost all jazz traditions (see below), but it nearly always takes place in the context of some larger structure that is planned in advance. This planning can be as simple as deciding who plays what when (the order of the solos, for example) and as complicated as a completely written-out arrangement in which most of the musicians are guided by notes printed on the page. At the very least, musicians will usually decide in advance the tune that will serve as the basis for their improvisations. Perhaps another way to put this is to think of jazz as a very "free" music, one that allows players to explore a variety of means of self-expression, but that at the same time, with freedom comes responsibility. Some type of underlying organization must be in place or the result is chaos.

Individuality vs. collectivity
From the very beginning of jazz's history, a premium has always been placed on musicians who create their own sound—one that is highly personal and instantly recognizable. Whereas classical musicians will learn the "correct" and "incorrect" ways to play their instruments, for the jazz musician, there is no "proper" way to make a sound. Though some jazz musicians

study their instruments in conservatories, many also learn simply by picking up an instrument and figuring out how to make a sound they like, whether or not it has anything to do with "acceptable" technique. The great New Orleans clarinetist and soprano saxophonist Sidney Bechet, for example, developed a totally idiosyncratic technique on his instrument—one that would make a classical musician cringe—simply by experimentation, but he had an enormous, rich, and passionate sound that was impossible to duplicate.

Many jazz musicians start their careers by copying another jazz musician outright (legions of saxophonists, for example, have learned Charlie Parker solos by heart) but at some point they must learn to develop their own voice or the music becomes stale. In fact, one of the most damning criticisms a jazz musician can levy at another is to say "he or she is just a Charlie Parker imitator." At the same time, all great jazz musicians are also good listeners, who take pleasure in what the fellow members of their group are trying to "say" with their instruments, and will often directly respond to ideas that are tossed out as part of an improvisation. In addition, all members of a jazz group pay close attention to how they sound *as a group;* brilliant solos are only as good as the context in which they are heard. Therefore, in any jazz performance there is always an interesting tension between attempts to sound like a true individual, as well to be a member of the "collective."

A few more specific features of the jazz tradition can be outlined, and many are related to the dualities discussed above.

1. **Improvisation**. Improvisation of some type is nearly always part of a jazz performance. Even if musicians are reading notes on a page, they can "improvise" through the way they attack or color a note, or the rhythmic impulse they bring to the music. In early jazz musicians often improvised by creating variations on a given melody. As the tradition developed, it became more common to use a *chord progression* as the basis for entirely new melodies. In more recent jazz traditions, even chords are abandoned and musicians will simply improvise on a scale, a motive, or even just a tonal center. No matter how they improvise, however, most musicians have a set of phrases (called "licks") that lie easily under their fingers and can be used and reused in a variety of contexts. Charlie Parker, for example, had many signature "licks" that make his style instantly recognizable. In other words, jazz musicians do often play musical lines they have played before, but where they place these lines, and how they play them, is part of the art of improvisation.

2. **Instrumentation**. Certain instruments have become strongly associated with the jazz tradition, mainly because of their tone color and ability to fit into an ensemble or carry a chord structure. And, from its earliest history, there has been a common division of some of the instruments into a subsection known as the "rhythm section" that maintains the rhythmic drive and reiterates the chord progression for other improvising musicians. Ensembles have continued to evolve, however, due to improvements in microphones and recording technology.

3. **The blues**. Nearly all jazz has some connection, even if subtle, with the African American blues tradition, in performance technique, common forms used, and overall musical "feel." In fact, there are those who would claim that when the music loses its connection to the blues, it ceases to be jazz. (This is the claim often used to prove that Kenny G. is *not* a jazz musician, even though he plays an instrument associated with jazz—the soprano saxophone—and improvises. His references to blues traditions, when they exist at all, are so stylized that they lack any strong connections to the genuine article.)

4. **Performance technique.** Largely out of the blues tradition comes the jazz player's proclivity for creating "new" sounds on his or her instrument, and using that instrument in an idiosyncratic way. Often these techniques mirror the use of the voice in various African American traditions; we know, for example, that the bending of pitches and growling or rasping sound often used by jazz musicians mirror black vocal traditions such as the blues, as well as both speech and singing in black church music. Listen to Louis Armstrong as both a vocalist and a trumpeter, and you will note there is little difference between the two. In addition, many people have likened the high pitches (usually out of the normal sound range of an instrument) associated with certain players such as saxophonist John Coltrane to "screams," even though they may reflect excitement or intensity on the part of the performer, rather than anguish. Such "screams" or "squeaks" are something to be carefully avoided in Western classical music, but many jazz musicians incorporate them into their improvisations intentionally.

5. **Rhythm.** Most jazz performances employ a subtle rhythmic sense that is often called "swing" or "swing feeling" (note this is a different meaning of the term than that used below to describe a style and era of jazz). This "swing feeling" is virtually impossible to define in words (one musician once noted: "if you gotta ask what swing is, you'll never know") but it is very different than the subtle pulse of most Western art music, the driving beat of popular music, or the dense polyrhythmic effect of many African traditions. Think of "swing" as a special kind of groove that is unique to jazz; it creates the subtle forward thrust of the music and often is what makes you tap your foot. Especially in the 1930s and 1940s, it was the "swing feeling" mastered by groups such as those led by Count Basie and Benny Goodman that made audiences leave their seats for the dance floor.

Brief History

The great sweep of jazz's first century is usually loosely divided into five general periods: (1) the music's origins and the emergence of its early masters; (2) the so-called "Swing Era" when the music was *the* popular music of the United States (and much of the world as well); (3) the emergence of bebop in the early 1940s; (4) the avant-garde movement of the late 1950s and early 1960s; and (5) the "fusion" movement of the 1970s and beyond, in which jazz absorbed influences from a variety of other musical traditions, including rock. Yet, though some categorization is necessary to make sense of this music's unique and fascinating path through history, such classifications must be used with care, for a newer style does not necessarily replace an older one. It is possible, in fact, to hear virtually any style of jazz being played in the 21st century; some musicians look back to the work of earlier performers, while others continue to push the music into new realms, often absorbing elements of other genres (including world music and hip-hop) along the way.

I. Early Jazz

Although New Orleans is often touted as "The Birthplace of Jazz," it is actually impossible to limit the music's emergence to a single geographic location. It is clear that vernacular music traditions that would feed into emerging jazz were developing throughout the country at the turn of the 19th century. Yet, New Orleans did supply a distinctive style of jazz, and most of the greatest early practitioners of the music (Louis Armstrong, Sidney Bechet, Ferdinand "Jelly Roll" Morton, and others) came from this vibrant cultural melting pot, where blues, classical music, ragtime, church music, and other traditions combined to help create the irresistible, largely improvised music that took the country by storm in the 1920s. The first recordings of jazz were actually made in in New York in 1917 by a white group, The Original Dixieland Jazz Band, an ensemble made up of Italian Americans from New Orleans, but the true birth of jazz recording is usually traced to the magnificent recordings made in 1923 by King Oliver and His Creole Jazz Band, in which Armstrong played second cornet to Oliver's lead. Joining the migration of many African Americans to northern cities during the so-called "Great Migration" from the South in the late teens and early 1920s, Oliver, Armstrong, Morton, and many other musicians built careers in Chicago, where the music flourished and some of the early masterpieces by Armstrong and Morton were recorded. Many of these performances include what has become known as "collective improvisation"—everyone appearing to improvise simultaneously in a densely polyphonic texture—though we now know that a considerable amount of planning went into these "improvisations." Armstrong, however, partly with the encouragement of his wife Lillian Hardin Armstrong, soon emerged as one of the greatest musicians in the country, and since his ground-breaking recordings of the mid and late 1920s, jazz has been largely considered (rightly or wrongly) an art that celebrates the virtuoso soloist.

II. The Swing Era

In the 1930s, New York City became the center of jazz activity, as it has remained to the present day. In addition, partly because of the huge demand for dance music (the country was in the midst of the Depression and dance—along with movies—provided escape from the dismal realities of daily life) and the sizeable venues into which jazz musicians were booked, jazz bands became larger, often with entire sections of reed and brass instruments. In addition, the saxophone—considered largely a joke instrument in the 1920s—emerged as the jazz instrument *par excellence* (perhaps because of its versatility and similarity to the human voice). This was the era of the jazz big band, and of groups such as those led by Duke Ellington, Benny Goodman, and Count Basie. It was also the heyday of the jazz arranger, who took on the responsibility of laying out specific parts for members of the band (often in notation) as well as incorporating improvisation, for collective music-making was no longer feasible in a group of 15 or more musicians. Many of the era's greatest soloists—saxophonists Coleman Hawkins, Lester Young, Johnny Hodges and Ben Webster, clarinetists Goodman and Artie Shaw, trumpeters Roy Eldridge, Red Allen and Cootie Williams (as well as Armstrong, of course)—played with these big bands. Big band jazz swept the nation, becoming the most popular type of dance music on the scene, and resulting in the creation of thousands of records. In addition, radio, which had begun to have an impact on American culture in the 1920s, exploded into one of the country's most important media.

III. Bebop

Largely because of financial hardships brought on by World War II, the popularity and economic feasibility of big band jazz began to wane in the 1940s. But a host of young musicians had already begun experimenting with new approaches to the music, whether out of boredom, a sense that African American musicians were being exploited in big bands, or simply the natural tendency of creative minds to evolve. These developments went largely undocumented, as they often took place in late-night, informal jam sessions. In addition, in the early 1940s the Musician's Union called for a ban on all recordings (in protest over the fact that musicians were not being recompensed for the airplay of their records), so the brewing sea change in jazz went largely unrecorded. Yet, by 1945 trumpeter Dizzy Gillespie and alto saxophonist Charlie "Bird" Parker, along with pianists Thelonious Monk and Bud Powell and drummers Max Roach and Kenny Clarke, had essentially redefined jazz. Though their music, which became known as "bebop," remained firmly rooted in past jazz traditions, they promoted a return to small-ensemble music, and greatly expanded jazz's harmonic, rhythmic and melodic possibilities. They also seemed to suggest that jazz be taken more seriously as an art form, rather than dance music (though Gillespie once commented, when a listener complained that he couldn't dance to bebop, "*YOU* can't dance to it!"). This music of 1940s created the foundation for nearly all modern jazz, and saw an important separation between the music and social dancing. In addition, the popularity of jazz began to be supplanted by the emerging idioms of R&B and R&R.

IV. The Avant-Garde
Jazz musicians continued to explore the terrain opened up by Parker and Gillespie and others during the 1950s. Some created music even farther distant from the popular and accessible music of the 1930s, while others tried to counteract what they saw as the more "cerebral" aspects of bebop by playing music more deeply rooted in the blues and gospel. In 1959, a group led by saxophonist and composer Ornette Coleman (which had been playing to small and largely hostile audiences on the West Coast) took their inventive styles to New York. Coleman's music often did away entirely with usual ideas of improvising on a melody or chord progression. The work of Coleman and his compatriots is often referred to as "Free Jazz" (the name of an album Coleman recorded in 1960) but the idiom was not quite as loose as the name suggests, with often a tonal center or motive providing an important organizing principle, and close dialogue between the various musicians a crucial feature of the music's overall effect. Nevertheless, Coleman's music, which also revolutionized the roles of the various instruments in the ensemble, was highly controversial, as was his own edgy, often harsh instrumental tone and idiosyncratic technique, which some saw as evidence of poor musical training. Some musicians rejected the new styles entirely, while others—most notably, perhaps, saxophonist John Coltrane—were strongly influenced by them. Even trumpeter Miles Davis, though reportedly not a fan of avant-garde jazz, seems to have incorporated some of its traits in the work of his famous 1960s quintet, which featured saxophonist Wayne Shorter, bassist Ron Carter, drummer Tony Williams, and pianist Herbie Hancock.

V. Fusion and Jazz-Rock
In 1969 Miles Davis made the highly controversial move of including electric instruments on his *In A Silent Way* and *Bitches Brew* albums, adding as well rhythmic structures aligned with rock and soul. Many accused Davis of "selling out"—of trying to pander to popular music tastes of the time—but though Davis was certainly interested in expanding his dwindling audience, he also heard fascinating possibilities in the work of Sly and the Family Stone, James Brown, and Jimi Hendrix. Many alumni from Miles's "electric" groups went on to form fusion bands of their own—keyboardist Chick Corea with Return to Forever, Wayne Shorter and keyboardist Joe Zawinul with Weather Report, guitarist John McLaughlin with The Mahavishnu Orchestra, and Herbie Hancock with a group that produced the hugely popular *Headhunters* album in 1973. Though many critics complained that their music "wasn't jazz," it did maintain improvisation and connections with the blues that had always been a part of the jazz tradition.

VI. The 1980s and Beyond
The last three decades have seen the extension of many of jazz history's streams, as well as the promotion of jazz as an art worthy of academic discourse. In the 1980s, New Orleans-born Wynton Marsalis, himself an alumnus of drummer Art Blakey's Jazz Messengers, emerged as one of the most important spokespersons for the music. Though widely criticized by many as musically conservative, he has done much for the promotion of jazz worldwide, especially in his role as director of Lincoln Center's jazz program. As it always has, the art of jazz continues to evolve and reflect changing political and economic climates, as well as absorbing other music that emerges in the now-digital age.

CHAPTER 8: WORLD MUSIC

Selected World Cultures and Repertories

We live in a time of unprecedented access to information about and exposure to cultures from all over the world. The scholarly study of human customs, languages, religious beliefs, social institutions, family life, and so on is the subject of anthropology. The scholarly investigation of the music of different cultures is called ethnomusicology, and encompasses learning about how, why, where, and when music is created, who performs it, and its distinctive features. The following sections provide an introduction to the rich, complex, and diverse musical cultures of four world areas: Africa, India, Indonesia, and the Caribbean.

Africa

Africa is the second largest continent in the world, and home to a tenth of the world's population and at least a thousand different indigenous languages. Therefore, it is impossible to describe a single entity called "African music." One need only compare the sacred music of the Gnawa musicians of Morocco with the choral traditions that arose in the townships of South Africa to see the vast range of musical practices found throughout this huge and complex region.

Especially during the last century, however, scholars have tried to find ways to talk in general ways about Africa's rich traditions, while always acknowledging the sometimes very subtle differences between countries and ethnic groups. Beyond the recognition that African musicians maintained a vibrant and very distinct art, it has also been noted that this music—especially that of West Africa, from where the majority of slaves were taken—has played a significant role in the black cultural Diaspora, with important implications for the music of Latin America, the Caribbean (see), and a variety of African American traditions (see American vernacular traditions; Jazz). Thus, understanding a few concepts that are shared by much African music helps listeners appreciate not only the continent's music itself but a host of related traditions. Fortunately, in today's digital age, recordings of music from virtually all corners of Africa—both traditional repertoires and styles influenced by Western popular music—are readily available.

The Sahara Desert, which takes up almost the entire northern third of the continent, is perhaps the most important dividing line that comes into play when discussing music in Africa. Countries that lie partly or entirely north of the Sahara (Egypt, Libya, Morocco, Tunisia, etc.) tend to share many qualities with music of the Middle East. The rainforests and grasslands of Sub-Saharan Africa (Ghana, Cameroon, The Congo, Zambia, etc.) have produced very different traditions. In addition, distinctions are often made between Sub-Saharan musical traditions of Western, Eastern, Central, and Southern Africa.

As different as African musical traditions may sound from each other, they do tend to share both cultural and musical elements. However, one must always be cautious when trying to view these traditions through a Western musical or aesthetic lens.

1. Music and dance. Linguistic scholars have been hard-pressed to find a single word that means "music" in many African languages. Music and bodily movement are usually considered part of a single whole, and sound cannot be separated from the cultural (and often religious) function of musical performances.

2. In many African cultures, music and dance are considered communal activities; the Western idea of sitting silently while a performance is taking place is an anathema to these traditions. Many musical techniques that are shared by African musics—particularly the idea of "call and response," where a soloist or group of performers will engage in short exchanges with other performers—seem to have arisen from this communal attitude toward music-making.

3. Oral traditions. Nearly all African traditions have been passed down orally, and their study by Western scholars has often involved the transcription of performances into Western musical notation, which often proves woefully inadequate for the job. The influx of Christian choral music, especially in the southern regions of Africa, has resulted in music somewhat more easily notatable, and some African musicians do now use the familiar five-line system to capture their art.

4. In many African traditions, rhythm—the way music moves through time—seems to be privileged over melody and harmony. Many African performances are highly polyphonic and made up of several layers of interlocking rhythmic ostinatos, which are combined to create an overall effect suitable for the religious or cultural ceremony for which the sounds are being produced.

5. Instruments. The variety of instruments found throughout Africa is astounding. Perhaps most impressive is the range of percussion instruments (both idiophones and membranophones) that are often combined with distinctive uses of the human voice. In listening to performances of African music, those of us immersed in the Western musical tradition may be initially drawn to the vocal line as the most prominent feature, yet it may just be one element of a larger, complex musical texture.

India

North Indian Classical Music (Hindustani sangita)

Music from the Indian subcontinent is one of the non-Western repertories that has fascinated Western musicians and audiences in recent decades. Improvisation is central to the performance of North Indian classical music (Hindustani music) and is mastered only after years of study with a guru. The skeletal elements from which the improvisation springs are the raga, an ascending and descending pattern of melodic pitches, and the tala, the organization of rhythm within a recurring cycle of beats. Rather than the 12-semitone octave of Western classical music, Indian music divides the octave into 22 parts. Although only some of those 22 pitches are used in a particular raga, the complexity and subtlety of Indian melody is attributable in part to this relatively large vocabulary of pitch material. With respect to temporal organization, Indian music organizes spans of time into cycles of beats, somewhat comparable to the Western concept of meter. But whereas Western composers have worked predominantly in a framework of time spans divided into repeated cycles of two, three, or four beats, the time span of a tala is comprised of units of variable length, for example, a 14-beat tala of four plus three plus four plus three beats. A tala may also be of enormous duration in comparison with a Western measure, which rarely exceeds a few seconds in length.

There are hundreds of talas and thousands of ragas. Each raga has specific extra-musical associations such as a color, mood, season, and time of day. These associations shape the performer's approach to and the audience's experience of an improvisation, which can last from a few minutes to several hours. Indian music also has an important spiritual dimension and its history is intimately connected to religious beliefs and practices. As stated by the great sitarist Ravi Shankar, "We view music as a kind of spiritual discipline that raises one's inner being to divine peacefulness and bliss. The highest aim of our music is to reveal the essence of the universe it reflects....Through music, one can reach God."

The typical texture in Indian music consists of three functionally distinct parts: (1) a drone, the main pitches of the raga played as a background throughout a composition; (2) rhythmic improvisations performed on a pair of drums; and (3) melodic improvisations executed by a singer or on a melody instrument. One of the most common melody instruments is the sitar, a plucked string instrument with a long neck and a gourd at each end, six or seven plucked strings, and nine to thirteen others that resonate sympathetically. The melody instrument or voice is traditionally partnered by a pair of tablas, two hand drums tuned to the main tones of the pitch pattern upon which the sitar melody is based. The drone instrument is often a tambura, a plucked string instrument with four or five strings each tuned to one tone of the basic scale and plucked to produce a continuous, unvarying drone accompaniment.

A raga performance traditionally opens with the alap, a rhapsodic, rhythmically free introductory section in which the melody instrument is accompanied only by the drone. Microtonal ornaments and slides from tone to tone are typical elements of a melodic improvisation. The entrance of the drums marks the second phase of the performance in which a short composed melodic phrase, the gat, recurs between longer sections of improvisation. Ever more rapid notes moving through extreme melodic registers in conjunction with an increasingly accelerated interchange of ideas between melody and drums produces a gradual intensification as the performance progresses to its conclusion.

South Indian Classical Music (Karnataka sangita)

South Indian classical music (Karnatic or Carnatic music) evolved from ancient Hindu traditions and is relatively free of the Arabic and Islamic influences that contribute to Hindustani music. Karnatic music is primarily vocal and the texts devotional in nature (often in Sanskrit). The instrumental music consists largely of performances of vocal compositions with a melody instrument replacing the voice and staying within a limited vocal range. It is important to note that the vocal style is so advanced that it seems almost instrumental in nature. One could say in Karnatic music that vocal and instrumental styles merge into one. Works in this tradition are normally composed, as opposed to the improvised Hindustani tradition, with new compositions being written every day. Four Karnatic composers of great importance are Purandara Dasa (1494–1564), Shayama Shastri (1762–1827), Tyagaraja (ca.1767–1848), and Muttusvami Dikshitar (1775–1835).

Karnatic music uses the same system of raga (scale) and tala (meter) as found in the north, but the systems for classifying raga and tala are more highly developed and consistent, thanks to a long period of growth with a minimum of influence from the outside.

Just as Hindustani instrumental music often follows the formal outline of an *alap* (slow meditative section exploring the raga), followed by a *gat* (faster section with percussion accompaniment), many Karnatic compositions are in the form Pallavi: (Opening Section), Anupallavi: (Middle Section), Charanam: (Concluding Section) with an abbreviated pallavi serving as a refrain between subsequent sections and concluding the piece. Towards the end of the composition an improvised section, called the *svara kalpana*, is often inserted where the vocalist expands on the pitches in the raga while singing with "sa re ga ma" syllables instead of the text. This improvised singing may alternate with a melody instrument, such as a violin, imitating the singer.

Two Western instruments have become a standard part of Karnatic music, the aforementioned violin for melodic use and the hand-pumped harmonium for playing the sustained drone pitches. A present-day concert ensemble might include a lead vocalist, a violin, a mridangam (a two-headed drum functioning as the tabla does in Hindustani music), a ghatam (a large mud pot reinforcing the tala) and one or two tambura (large string instruments performing the drone pitches).

Indonesia

The Republic of Indonesia consists of a string of about 6,000 islands, including Java, Sumatra, New Guinea, and Bali, that lie between the Indian and Pacific Oceans. The main instrumental ensemble of Indonesia is the gamelan, a percussion ensemble of up to 80 musicians that accompanies ceremonial plays, religious rituals, community events, and dancing in Indonesia. All gamelan traditions are rooted in Hindu-Buddhism, and gamelan performance is deeply connected with rituals. Gamelan instruments can be made of wood and bamboo, but the ensemble's distinctive sound derives from the preponderance of instruments made of bronze—large tuned gongs, kettles of various sizes, and bars of different lengths in a xylophone-like arrangement. The instruments are themselves charged with charismatic power and are often intricately carved and brilliantly painted with figures and designs that replicate elements of the universe. In Bali, gamelans belong to village communities, in Java also to families and the state.

Each gamelan composition is based on one fixed and unique melody, in Java *balungan*, in Bali *pokok*. There are thousands of these melodies, which have been passed on mainly through oral transmission. The melodic material is derived from numerous ways of dividing the octave into five or seven pitches, thereby producing a variety of scales. In the course of a performance, the performers execute highly complex variations, with the tempo of the ensemble controlled by drummers playing interlocking rhythmic patterns. The resulting layers of related melodies, which coincide at points punctuated by the sound of huge gongs, mirror the overlapping and interweaving of cosmological forces.

China

The People's Republic of China occupies a vast land area and is the world's most populous nation. It is also one of the earliest centers of civilization, as evidenced by religious and philosophical texts, novels and poetry, scientific literature, and musical instruments that survive from the early dynastic era (beginning in 1122 BC). In the sixth century BC Confucius wrote about the value of music to man in achieving the goals of living in harmony with nature and maintaining a well regulated society. Although Chinese systems of notation can be dated back to the fourth century BC, most Chinese music has been passed on orally.

Over the course of China's long history, different districts evolved distinctive linguistic dialects and cultural practices, including those associated with music. One tradition that is common throughout China is that all theater is musical and all regions maintain companies of singers and instrumentalists for theatrical performances. Peking Opera is the form of Chinese musical drama best known in the West and has enjoyed great popularity both at court and among common people in China. The stories, of which there are over 1,000, deal mainly with social and romantic relationships and military exploits. Staging is without sets and props and, until the 1920s, all roles were sung by men and boys.

Notable features of Peking Opera are its repertory of subtle and highly stylized physical movements and gestures and a tight, nasal vocal timbre. The singers are accompanied by an orchestra consisting of strings, winds, and percussion which, in the Chinese system, are classified according to the materials from which they are made – metal, stone, earth/clay, skin, silk, wood, gourd, and bamboo. Among China's important instruments are the erhu and ching-hu, both bowed strings; the cheng and ch'in, plucked strings; the lute-like pipa; the ti-tzu, a transverse flute made of bamboo; the double-reed so-na; and a wide array of gongs, chimes, bells, drums, cymbals, and clappers. The "conductor" of a Peking Opera orchestra is one of the percussionists, who sets the beat for the ensemble.

The music of Peking Opera exemplifies three characteristic features: 1) pentatonic scale, in which the octave is divided into five steps, producing a scale whose intervallic distances approximate the whole step and step-and-a-half of the Western system; 2) monophonic texture, one melody performed by both singer and instrumentalists, although in different octaves; 3) heterophony, a performance practice whereby the players spontaneously and simultaneously introduce variants of the melody, sometimes producing brief moments of improvised polyphony.

That these features are also found in the music of Japan and Korea is indicative of China's contact with other cultures of Asia, sometimes through military conquest. China also maintained naval and overland caravan routes for trading with Eastern Europe, the Middle East, Southeast Asia, the Indian subcontinent, and the countries along the Adriatic and Mediterranean. A 19th century German geographer dubbed this network the Silk Road. European influence on Chinese music was especially strong during the Republic of China period, 1912-1949, when Chinese musicians went to Europe to study, Western-style orchestras were established, Western notation was adopted, and Western harmonies were added to traditional Chinese folk music.

Following the establishment in 1949 of the People's Republic of China under Chairman Mao Zedong, the role of music was to promote the ideology of China's communist party. The spheres of musical activity were particularly restricted during the Cultural Revolution, 1966-1976, when China entered an isolationist period. The evils of capitalism and the bourgeois and decadent values of Western culture were denounced, and intellectuals and members of professional classes were sent to the country to be "re-educated." Since the 1980s, the revival of traditional Chinese musical practices and repertories, and renewed contact between the musicians of China and the rest of the world are important manifestations of the modern phenomenon of globalization and cross-cultural exchange.

The Caribbean

Stretching from Cuba, located only 90 miles south of Florida, east and south to Trinidad, just off the coast of South America, the Caribbean is one of the most culturally diverse and musically rich regions of the world. Spanish conquest and settlement in the 17th century wiped out most of the native Carib people. English, French, and Dutch settlement followed and sugar production became the primary industry of the area. In order to operate the labor-intensive sugar plantations, millions of African slaves were imported during the 17th, 18th, and early 19th centuries. When slavery was abolished, large numbers of East Indians came to English-speaking islands to work the sugar plantations. Today each island has its own mix of European, African, and Asian populations. Haiti, for example, is predominantly African, while Puerto Rico boasts a mix of African and Spanish people, and Trinidad is nearly evenly split between citizens of African and East Indian ancestry. Reflecting this diverse population, the islands have developed a wide range of distinctive linguistic, religious, culinary, and musical traditions.

The concept of *creolization* is essential to understand the music and culture of the Caribbean. Creolization refers to the development of a distinctive new cultural form resulting from contact between two or more different cultures. Throughout the Caribbean, the blending of African and European (and occasionally East Indian) cultures has led to the emergence of new forms of language, religion, food, and of course music. With regard to music, African concepts of polyrhythm, call-and-response singing, repetition and subtle variation, along with use of percussion instruments (particularly skin drums) have blended with European melodies, harmonic accompaniment, verse/chorus song structure, and use of string and brass instruments. The diversity of Caribbean folk musical styles may be organized on a stylistic continuum, with neo-African drumming and ritual song/chant on one end, and European sounding hymn singing, military marches, social dance music, and lyrical ballads on the other. In between lie an array of truly mixed, creolized song/dance forms including the *son* of Cuba, the *plena* of Puerto Rico, the *meringue* of the Dominican, the *mento* of Jamaica, and the *calypso* of Trinidad.

During the 20th century independence, urbanization, and emigration, along with a decline in the sugar industry and the rise of tourism, have brought sweeping changes to the Caribbean cultural landscape. The rise of mass media and international travel resulted in further mixing of Caribbean music with American and African popular styles, resulting in modern pop dance forms such as the Cuban/Puerto Rican/NYC *salsa*, Trinidadian *socca*, Jamaican *reggae*, Haitian *konpa*, and *zouk* from Martanique and Guadeloupe. Many of these styles have become popular in urban centers outside of the Caribbean with large populations of Island immigrants such as New York, Miami, and London. Today New York City's dance and concert halls feature the top salsa, meringue, reggae, konpa, and socca stars, and Brooklyn's Labor Day West Indian Carnival has grown into the largest ethnic outdoor festival in the United States.

Jibaro, Bomba, *and* Plena *Music of Puerto Rico*

There are three primary folk music genres indigenous to the Island of Puerto Rico. These are the Spanish-derived *jibaro* music associated with the small farms and interior mountain communities, and the *bomba* and *plena* styles identified with the coastal towns with larger African populations.

Because Puerto Rico's agricultural economy was centered in coffee and tobacco and not the labor-intensive sugar industry that dominated most of the Caribbean, fewer African slaves were imported and the influence of Spanish culture remained strong. The *jibaros*, the Spanish descendents who worked the interior farms, developed their own song and dance forms based heavily on Spanish traditions. Elite dance music and poetry, imported from Europe by the wealthy landowners, or *hacendados*, along with Spanish folk traditions, found their way into the jibaros repertoires. The *seis* is song set in 10-line verse form with lyrics dealing with idealized love, motherhood, the suffering of the jibaro farmer, and the beauty of the Puerto Rican countryside. Another song form, the *aguinaldo*, is associated specifically with the Christmas season. The seis and aguiandlo may be sung in a slow, ballad style, or played in a livelier tempo when used to accompany dancing at jibaro fiestas. A typical jibaro ensemble consists of guitar, *cuatro* (a guitar with five doubled strings), maracas, and guiro scraper, backing a *trovador* (singer/poet) who sings stock verses and improvises *decimas* (10-line text stanzas) on the spot. Jibaro singing is characterized by a high, tense, dramatic vocal delivery.

In coastal towns like Ponce, where African slaves were brought to work the sugar plantations, *bomba* and *plena* music developed. *Bomba*, the most African-influenced Puerto Rican folk style, features exuberant call-and-response singing between a leader and a chorus, interlocking drum patterns, and intense drummer/dance interaction (the latter responds to the lead drummer's improvised rhythms). A typical *bomba* ensemble consists of a pair of sticks known as *fúa* or *cua* that provide a steady ground beat when struck on a hard surface; a maraca; and two or more barrel-shaped drums. The lyrics to *bomba* songs usually refer to everyday work and social events.

Plena is a creolized folk song that combines African-derived call (leader) and response (chorus) singing, drumming, and dance with European-derived melodies and harmonies. A traditional *plena* ensemble includes several handheld frame drums called *panderetas* (similar to a tambourine but without the metal jingles), the *güiro* (scraped gourd), and one or more melodic instruments such as the accordion, harmonica, or *cuatro*. Often referred to as "*el periodico cantado*" (the sung newspaper), *plena* songs relate current and historical events of community life. In recent years the plena ensembles have incorporated horns, keyboards, electric bass, and extended percussion to produce a more modern dance sound.

Carnival Music from Trinidad and Brooklyn

Trinidad, the small Caribbean island nation located just off the coast of Venezuela, is home to one of the world's largest carnivals. New World urban carnivals have their immediate roots in the pre-Lenten celebrations of medieval and Renaissance Europe. On such occasions large numbers of the people took to the streets to frolic and engage in satirical performances that often challenged social hierarchy and everyday order. When Euro-Catholic carnival practices were transplanted to the New World by French, Spanish, and Portuguese settlers, they mixed and mingled with the traditions of the African slaves and their descendants, resulting in the emergence of spectacular creolized celebrations in cities such as Rio de Janeiro, Brazil; Port of Spain, Trinidad; and New Orleans. Increasingly these festivities took on an African flavor, as African masking traditions and neo-African music styles featuring call-and-response singing, improvisation, and syncopated dance rhythms became hallmarks of urban carnival.

The development of carnival in Port of Spain, Trinidad, demonstrates this process. The original 18th-century pre-Lenten street processions of the French planters were eventually taken over by the island's African population who blended their own emancipation celebrations into the European festivities. By the mid-19th century they had established a large-scale annual celebration in the days leading up to Ash Wednesday. Street rituals evolved around groups of masqueraders who paraded and danced to percussion ensembles and a chantwell who led the revelers in rowdy call-and-response singing that became an important source of modern-day *calypso* song. By the early post–World War II years ensembles of steel pan players (steelbands) became the main source of music for the street processions of carnival masqueraders (mas bands).

By the turn of the 20th century the noisy call-and-response street carnival singing developed into calypso songs characterized by lyrical melodies, bouncy syncopated rhythms, and a solo verse/chorus refrain structure. Drums and bamboo percussion instruments were replaced by string (usually guitar) and horn accompaniments. Calypso songs offered witty and satirical commentary on a wide range of social issues, current events, and lewd scandals, often mocking the pretensions of the upper classes. In the 1930s a number of calysponians boasting titles like Lord Invader, the Duke of Iron, Houdini, and Roaring Lion traveled to New York to record and perform. Eventually they would foment a calypso craze in the United States that culminated with Harry Belafonte's 1957 hit, "Day-O." By the late 1970s Trinidadian calypso singers were incorporating elements of American disco and soul music into their sound to forge the new style of soca (soul/calypso), which featured a pounding bass line, heavy drums, and riffing synthesizers. Soca lyrics, often based around simple choruses exhorting listeners to party and dance, generally lacked the sophisticated wit and sardonic commentary associated with earlier calypso songs.

The second important Trinidadian carnival tradition, steel pan music, grew out of 19th and early 20th century drum and bamboo percussion ensembles that accompanied singers and costumed revelers in carnival street processions. Sometime in the mid-1930s *tamboo bamboo* percussion ensembles began experimenting with paint and trash cans, automobile brake drums, and other metal objects. Players eventually discovered that different pitches could be achieved by pounding the bottoms of metal containers into different shapes and striking them with sticks. Following WW II, the first true steel drums were forged by pan tuners (builders) who cut oil drums into different sizes to produce a wider tonal range. More sophisticated techniques were developed for grooving notes, leading to pans capable of producing fully chromatic scales and conventional Western harmonies. By the 1950s steel pan orchestras were playing complex arrangements of calypsos as well as Latin dance music, American pop songs, and European classical pieces.

Steel orchestras grew in size, and today may number as many as 100 performers playing a range of pans divided into six or seven sections. The high-range tenor pans usually play the primary melodic line while the double tenors and double seconds double the melody or contribute second melodies. The mid-range cello and guitar pans provide chordal accompaniment. Full-sized, fifty-five gallon drums, arranged in six, nine, or twelve drum configurations, maintain a moving bass line. A trap drum set, one or more conga drums, an iron (automobile brake drum struck with a metallic stick), and additional hand percussion provide a dense rhythmic accompaniment for dancing.

Brooklyn's West Indian Carnival, based on the Trinidad model, is the most recent urban carnival to rise to prominence. Originally staged in Harlem on Labor Day (in deference to NYC's climate that would not allow for a large-scale outdoor festivities during the traditional mid-winter, pre-Lenten carnival season), West Indian Carnival moved to central Brooklyn's Eastern Parkway in the late 1960s where large numbers of West Indians were settling following the 1965 immigration reforms. Mas bands of fancy costumed carnival-goers dance to steel bands and sound trucks pumping out contemporary calypso and soca hits as well Jamaican reggae, Haitian konpa, and the latest pop music offerings from Grenada, Barbados, and Panama. By the 1990s Brooklyn Carnival had evolved into the largest ethnic festival in the United States, drawing an estimated two million people. The festivities stretch over the entire Labor Day weekend with a series of nightly concerts headlined by international calypso and reggae stars, fancy costume competitions, and a panorama contest featuring the borough's top steel bands.

South America

Until fairly recently, there had been a tendency to see the cultural traditions of the massive South American continent as monolithic. However, in the 1960s scholars began to unravel the area's rich tapestry of musical cultures and practices, and with the increase in recordings, the public is better able to appreciate the variety of musical traditions found here.

As many as 117 languages are spoken in the continent, in perhaps 2000 different dialects. Until the 16th century, South America boasted some of the world's most sophisticated cultures (the most famous being, perhaps, the Incas of the Andean regions). In the 1530s, the Spanish conquistadors arrived, followed by the Portuguese. They brought with them elements of European culture, as well as Catholicism, but a variety of diseases as well that devastated parts of the indigenous population.

Some indigenous traditions have remained nearly untouched until quite recently, because of the geographical remoteness of the cultures that created them (vast areas of rainforest and mountain terrain had remained unexplored until quite recently). But for the most part, South American music is a fascinating mix of Spanish, Portuguese, and indigenous art forms, as well as the music of Africans who were brought to the continent as slaves. Repertories can be as diverse as the *romanzas* found throughout South America (historically linked to folk songs of the Spanish renaissance) and the music of the Brazilian *capoeira* tradition, an art form strongly influenced by African music that is accompanied by physical movements resembling martial arts.

Argentina and *Tango*

In music of both its indigenous peoples and that of the Spanish conquistadors of the 16th century, as well as more recent immigrants, Argentina boasts a rich and varied heritage of art, folk, and popular traditions. Perhaps the musical genre most closely associated with this diverse country of nearly forty million is the *tango*. In fact, few artistic expressions are so closely associated with their country of origin as the tango is with Argentina, though variations of this popular dance arose in many Latin American countries. Perhaps no other proof is necessary than the fact that the climactic song "Don't Cry For Me, Argentina," from Andrew Lloyd Webber's *Evita*, is cast in a tango style.

As both a seductive dance and a musical genre, tango had lowly origins in the brothels of Buenos Aires, Argentina's capital city, where it took shape during the last three decades of the 19th century, drawing on a variety of earlier Spanish and Creole forms. However, by the turn of the century, the dance and its music had begun to be accepted by the urban middle class, and been exported to the world. In the early 1910s, tango, perhaps because of its aura of the risqué (in its most popular form it is a couples dance, with the dancers tightly clasped together, and the male performing stylized moves that suggest erotic power and conquest) created a sensation in Europe and the United States. As a result, any music with the tango's characteristic "habanera" rhythm (think of the title character's famous aria in Bizet's opera *Carmen*) began to be called a "tango," though true Argentinean tango continued to develop as a distinctive art form.

The earliest tango ensembles were made up simply of violin, flute and guitar, though the guitar was occasionally replaced by an accordion. The turn of the century saw the incorporation of the *bandoneón*, a special type of 38-key accordion, as well as the piano. Later groups brought in additional string instruments, including the double bass. By the time of tango's "Golden Age" in the 1940s, some ensembles had grown to the size of small orchestras, with full string sections, several bandoneónes, and often vocalists.

By the late 1950s and early 1960s, the popularity of tango in its native Argentina had been largely eclipsed by newer forms of popular and folk music. But with the rise in popularity of composer and bandoneón virtuoso Astor Piazzolla (1921-1992) and his "New Tango" (see Musician Biographies), tango reached a new international audience, culminating in the wildly successful world tour of the Tango Argentino show, a stage extravaganza created in the early 1980s by Claudio Segovia and Hector Orezzoli that eventually made its way to Broadway.

Jewish Klezmer Music

Klezmer music is a term used to designate the Yiddish dance music of Ashkenazi Jews that dates back to the Middle Ages when it developed in Eastern Europe before eventually migrating to the United States. The Yiddish term "klezmer" comes from two Hebrew words, klei-zemer, which translates as "vessel of melody."

Early Klzemer bands played for a variety of social occasions including weddings, holiday celebrations, and rite of passage ceremonies throughout European Jewish communities. Up through the 18th century fiddles, cellos, string basses, flutes, drums, and tsimbls (hammered dulcimers) were the primary instruments. By the early 19th century the clarinet became the primary lead melodic instrument, and brass instruments including the trumpet, trombone, and tuba were added to the ensembles. Repertories were wide, including Yiddish melodies, Hassidim chants and dances tunes, non-Jewish dance forms such as the polka, light classical pieces, and salon dances such as the waltz.

Klzemer tunes are most often built around 8 or 16 bar, AB or ABC sections that are repeated with small variations. Melodic lines tend to be modal with complex ornamentations resulting from the generous use of trills, slurs, slides, and triplets. The clarinet is known for its particularly wild, shrill sounds (the dramatic clarinet glissando that opens George Gershwin's *Rhapsody in Blue* is thought to be influenced by klezmer styling). Harmonic accompaniments are characteristically built around minor chords; often a piece will feature dramatic shifts between minor and major modalities. Most klezmer dance pieces have a strong rhythmic pulse stressing the downbeat of a 2/4 or 4/4 meter producing a bouncy feel. Occasionally irregular meters such as 3/8 or 9/8 are used. Klezmer tunes sometimes begin with a taxim, or free meter modal improvisation, usually played on the clarinet.

Social and political unrest in Russia, Poland, and other regions of Eastern Europe fostered the immigration of millions of Yiddish-speaking, Ashkenazi Jews to America in the late nineteenth and early twentieth centuries, most of whom settled in New York City. Klezmer music became popular at Jewish-American weddings, holiday celebrations and social club dances, and by the 1920s was being recorded by Jewish musicians like virtuoso clarinetist Dave Tarras. Born in the Ukraine into a family of musicians, Tarras immigrated to New York in 1922 and became the leading klezmer clarinetist of his generation. In the tradition of the old world klezmer bands, early New York Jewish ensembles consisted of reeds, brass, and string instruments, often backed by accordion or piano and drum accompaniment. As Jewish musicians came under the influence of American tin pan alley and early jazz of the 1920s and 1930s they created innovative hybrids like Yiddish swing and the popular Yiddish theater songs.

Interest in traditional Asheknazi culture in general and klezmer music in particular waned during the Holocaust, World War Two, and the early post-War years. The 1970s saw a revival of activity by a new generation of Jewish musicians bent on rediscovering the roots of their Ashekanazi ancestors. Not surprisingly, New York was the center of the action, and at the forefront of the revival was Brooklyn-born clarinet virtuoso Andy Statman (b. 1950). A protégé of Dave Tarras, Statman spent years mastering the traditional klezmer style and repertoire. His eclectic tastes have led him to incorporate elements of bluegrass, jazz, rock, Middle Eastern music, and Western classical music into his innovative sound. Today klezmer has become a true world music, blending the traditional Asheknazi tunes of Eastern Europe with the sounds of modern classical, jazz, rock, soul, rap, and various North African and Mid-Eastern musics.

APPENDIX 1: MUSICIAN BIOGRAPHIES

Anderson, Laurie (b. 1947)

Born in Chicago, performance artist Laurie Anderson studied both art and the violin until age 16 when she decided to stop playing the instrument in order to focus on art and literature. Her passion for reading and art led her to Barnard College where she studied art history. After graduation she studied with Carl Andre and Sol LeWitt at the School of Visual Arts and completed an M.F.A. in sculpture from Columbia University in 1972. Music became a part of Anderson's work in her 1973 performance *Automotive* (a concert for "nice cars in harmony") and she returned to the violin (although in an unconventional way) in 1975 when she invented the tape bow violin by replacing the violin strings with a tape recorder playback head and the bow hair with a prerecorded piece of magnetic tape. Sound was produced as she dragged the magnetic tape bow back and forth over the playback head.

Anderson achieved popular success in 1981, and a recording contract with Warner Brothers Records, when her song *O Superman* (from Part 2 of her seven hour theater piece United States) was released as a single and climbed to number 2 on the British pop charts. An unlikely popular hit with a duration of over eight minutes, it is a typical Anderson composition in that it tells a story interjected with clichés (Pay as you go), slogans (Neither snow nor rain nor gloom of night...), and humorous asides (Hi Mom!). A political work, Anderson wrote the piece as a reaction to Iran-Contra, but it took on new meaning for her when she sang the lines "Here come the planes. They're American planes. Made in America." at Town Hall in New York City on September 19, 2001, ten days after the destruction of the World Trade Center.

Armstrong, Louis (1901–1971)

Cornetist, trumpeter, singer, and entertainer. An early nickname was "Dipper" (or "Dippermouth") and somewhat later (and more famously) "Satchelmouth" or "Satchmo," both references not just to physical characteristics but to the hugeness of his sound. Armstrong was one of the most important figures in the history of jazz. He was born in perhaps the worst slum of New Orleans, but surrounded from an early age by the rich and varied musical culture of that unique city. As a youngster he sang as part of a vocal quartet, and his first instrument was reportedly a tin horn given him by a Jewish family he worked for.

After being arrested in 1912 for firing a pistol on New Year's Eve, he was sent to the Home for Colored Waifs, where he began playing the cornet and had his first musical training. During his later teen years, Armstrong began playing with trombonist Kid Ory's Jazz Band, and in 1922 moved to Chicago where he joined the band of King Oliver, with whom he played second cornet. In 1924 he traveled to New York to play with Fletcher Henderson's band, a stint that had a startling impact on the large-ensemble jazz played in that city. In 1925, back in Chicago, he began a series of recordings under his own name that would become classics of early jazz ("Hotter Than That," "West End Blues," "Weather Bird," and many others). By the end of the Twenties he had emerged as perhaps the greatest trumpeter in jazz, and is largely credited for jazz's evolution from a collective style to a soloist's art. In 1929 he moved to New York, and in the next decade became an international superstar.

His appearance in almost 20 films and State Department-sponsored tours in the 1950s and 1960s brought jazz to international audiences and earned him the nickname "Ambassador Satch." Though he always considered himself first and foremost an entertainer, his solo trumpet playing is remarkable for its brilliance and virtuosity, hot tone, and fluid rhythmic sense.

The rough, gravelly quality of his voice (in many ways similar to his trumpet technique) is instantly recognizable and his dazzling vocal improvisations using nonsense syllables, called "scatting," became widely imitated. Among his hits as a singer toward the end of his career were "What a Wonderful World" (featured in the movie *Good Morning Vietnam*), "Mac the Knife," and especially "Hello, Dolly," the immense popularity of which took him utterly by surprise (the song knocked the Beatles out of first place on the pop charts in 1964). Armstrong's generosity was legendary, and in later years he could often be found on the steps of his home in Corona, Queens (now a museum), playing his horn with neighborhood kids.

Bach, Johann Sebastian (1685–1750)

Johann Sebastian Bach was the most illustrious member of a musical dynasty in which his ancestors for several generations had been musicians and three of his own 20 children were important composers and performers. Bach began his professional career at 18 when he was appointed to the court orchestra at Weimar in Germany. Over the next 20 years he held positions as organist, composer, and musical director in other north German cities, finally accepting the post as head of music at one of the major churches in Leipzig, where he remained until his death.

In some respects Bach was a provincial composer who spent his entire life in towns and moderate-size cities of northern Germany at a time when the great musical centers of Europe were London, Paris, Rome, Naples, and Venice. Moreover, although his creative output was vast, very few of his works were published during his lifetime. But while he was relatively unknown, he was both aware of and profoundly interested in the music of his predecessors and contemporaries. As a young man he walked 200 miles to experience at first hand the music of the aging organist and composer Dietrich Buxtehude. His justification for the three-month absence from his job was that he needed to "comprehend one thing and another about his art." A major reason for his move to Leipzig in 1723 was the cultural and educational opportunities available to himself and his family in a university city. Bach's large library of scores and theoretical writings also attests to the wide range of his musical interests, from Italian keyboard collections of the early Baroque to works by such contemporaries as the Frenchman Francois Couperin and the Italian Antonio Vivaldi. He also owned many writings on theological subjects, including the complete works of Martin Luther.

The relatively limited reputation Bach achieved during his lifetime was primarily as an organ virtuoso. In one contemporary account his playing on the pedals, for which he was especially renowned, was described as follows:

> Bach deserves to be called the miracle of Leipzig as far as music is concerned. For if it pleases him, he can by the use of his feet alone (while his fingers do either nothing or something else) achieve such an admirable, lively, and rapid concord of sounds on the church organ that others would seem unable to imitate with their fingers. He ran over the pedals as if his feet had wings, making the organ resound with a fullness of sound that penetrated the ears of those present like a thunderbolt. Frederick, Prince of Cassel admired him with such astonishment that he drew a precious ring from his finger and gave it to Bach as soon as the sounds had died away. If Bach earned such a gift for the agility of his feet, what, I ask, would the Prince have given him if he had called his hands into service as well?

Unfortunately, many of Bach's compositions that were preserved only in manuscript were lost in the years after his death. Nevertheless, the scholarly edition of his known surviving works fills almost 50 large volumes and a project to record them all in commemoration of the 300th anniversary of his birth in 1985 produced over 100 CDs. He made major contributions to every genre of the time except opera, and had he lived in a major cosmopolitan area with an opera house, he would undoubtedly have composed operas as well.

The duties and circumstances of the different positions Bach held largely dictated the focus of his compositional activity. Thus, many of his works for organ date from the periods when he was a church organist, those for instrumental ensemble from when he served Prince Leopold of Anhalt-Cothen as director of chamber music, and his Lutheran church music from his 27 years as cantor and director of music of the four principal churches of Leipzig. The music for the Leipzig Sunday services, which began at 7 A.M. and lasted about three hours, included an organ prelude and postlude by Bach, often improvised, congregational singing of hymns selected by Bach, and a multi-movement cantata by Bach for soloists, choir, and instrumentalists on a text appropriate to that Sunday in the church calendar. In addition to providing music for church services and civic events, Bach's responsibilities included the musical training of the town's professional musicians, and daily instruction of the boys at the boarding school attached to the St. Thomas Church. Teaching was an important activity of Bach's professional life and a number of his compositions were at least partly didactic. On the title of page of one of his important collections of keyboard music, the first volume of *The Well-Tempered Clavier*, Bach writes that he has composed the 24 preludes and fugues "For the Use and Profit of Musical Youth Desirous of Learning as well as for the Pastime of those Already Skilled in this Study."

Bach's thousands of surviving works are considered pinnacles of the art of polyphony, the musical texture consisting of the interweaving of two or more independent but simultaneous melodies. As described by a contemporary:

> The strands of his harmony are really concurrent melodies. They flow easily and expressively, never engross the hearer's attention, but divide his interest as now one, now the other becomes prominent. The combination of several melodies obliges the composer to use devices which are unnecessary in homophonic music. A single melody can develop as it pleases. But when two or more are combined each must be so delicately and cleverly fashioned that it can be interwoven with the others in this direction and that.

There is considerable documentary evidence that Bach's astonishing mastery of contrapuntal procedures was apparent not only in the works that survive in notation but in his ability to create complex polyphonic works extemporaneously. One famous incident occurred toward the end of his life when he was visiting his son, a musician at the court of the Prussian monarch Frederick the Great. Bach asked the king, who loved music and was a fairly accomplished flutist, to "give him a subject for a Fugue, in order to execute it immediately without any preparation. The King admired the learned manner in which his subject was thus executed extempore." Upon returning to Leipzig, Bach wrote out a series of contrapuntal elaborations on the royal theme that demonstrate every aspect of the art of counterpoint and dedicated them to the king with the title "Musical Offering."

Bach may have lived and worked in relative obscurity, but many of his contemporaries who achieved fame and celebrity during their lifetimes are now considered minor figures while Bach is regarded as one of the greatest musical geniuses of all time.

Bartok, Bela (1881–1945)

Bela Bartok was born in an area of Hungary that is now the westernmost tip of Romania. He began piano lessons at age five and in 1899 was admitted to the Budapest Academy of Music to study piano and composition. After his graduation in 1903, he embarked on a career unusually wide-ranging in its scope and impact. He was a concertizing pianist; a teacher of piano and member of the faculty of the Budapest Academy of Music; an internationally known composer; and a pioneer in the study of Eastern European folk music. In the 1930s, Bartok was among the many intellectuals and artists who came under attack for their protests against fascism and in 1940 he emigrated to the United States, where he continued to perform, teach, compose, and pursue his ethnomusicological research until his death.

Ethnomusicology is the scientific study of music of oral tradition, encompassing tribal and folk music and the art music produced by various world cultures. The discipline, whose origins date back to the 1880s, draws on methodologies of musicology, the scholarly study of Western art music, and anthropology, whose subject is mankind and human culture. Throughout the history of Western music, art and folk music repertories have influenced and enriched each other. The conscious exploitation of folk materials was especially important among 19th-century composers involved in the nationalist movement, who sought to imbue their music with a folk flavor by incorporating folk-like elements and even quoting actual folk melodies. But to Bartok and other ethnomusicologists, folk music was not a source of exotic atmosphere but an expression of human culture worth documenting for its inherent value. Beginning in his early twenties, Bartok and his friend and fellow musician Zoltan Kodaly made numerous expeditions to remote parts of Hungary and neighboring Slavic regions, recording on wax cylinders thousands of peasant tunes. As recalled by one of the singers they recorded:

> I was a girl. It happened one Sunday…. The professors…asked my mother to receive them and to agree to my singing into the gramophone for them. They called the machine a 'gramophone.' I sang one nice verse, and then another one. It came back sounding so beautiful. The whole village gathered around us. The whole village. Everyone was wanting to sing. The young men sang, the old women sang…. I remember that the professors asked me not to sing songs we'd learned from the soldiers, but only those from the mountain region here. So I only sang ones from the mountains.

From these recordings, the music and text of the songs were notated, analyzed, and codified. Bartok's published transcriptions of *Twenty Hungarian Folksongs* in 1906 was followed in 1908 by the first of his many musico-ethnological studies based upon his folk song research. He also composed numerous arrangements of folk songs—for piano, for voice and piano, for chorus—often publishing his settings alongside the notations of the tunes as recorded from the folk singers.

Bartok's folk music studies were seminal in the formulation of a strikingly personal language in which compositional practices of art music are fused with melodic, rhythmic, and harmonic materials of Eastern European folk music. Bartok was himself conscious of this profound influence, which he acknowledged in his many lectures and writings about his research and experiences in the field of folk music. As described by a scholar of Bartok's music:

> His music was nourished by his folkloristic studies while the scientific profited by the musician's experience in both theoretical and practical issues. Viewing it from this angle Bartok was a very rare combination of scientist and artist….And Bartok himself considered his folk music research as entirely equal in importance to his creative activity as a composer.

That creative activity encompassed a broad range of musical genres—opera and ballet; orchestral, chamber, and solo piano works; songs and choral compositions. It is in the design and character of Bartok's melodies, rhythms, textures, and harmonies that the influence of Eastern European folk music is most apparent. Bartok's ethnographic music studies brought him in contact with melodies based on scales other than major and minor, which is evident in the modal flavor of many of his works. His use of irregular accents derives from the practice he encountered of grouping rhythms not into repeated patterns of two's and three's but into five's, seven's and other combinations of two's and three's. His textures reflect performance practices in many folk-music traditions that involve the addition of drone accompaniments and improvised countermelodies created through heterophony and parallel motion. And Bartok creates sonorities based on pitch combinations characteristic of Eastern European music in addition to those traditionally employed in Western classical music

Beethoven, Ludwig Van (1770–1827)

Ludwig van Beethoven was born in Bonn, an important intellectual and cultural center in Germany and the seat of a court that flourished with particular brilliance in the late 18th century. Beethoven's father, a court musician, recognized his son's unusual musical gifts and sought to exploit them to his own advantage. Yet despite his scheming, which included representing Beethoven as two years younger than he actually was, and despite the boy's extraordinary talents, Beethoven never achieved wide acclaim as a child wonder as had Mozart a couple of decades earlier. Indeed, it was not until after Beethoven had permanently settled in Vienna in 1792 that he earned public recognition, initially as a virtuoso pianist, and later as a composer.

Contemporary accounts of Beethoven's playing stress especially the compelling emotion of his performance and his spectacular improvisations. In the words of one witness:

> His improvisation was most brilliant and striking. He knew how to achieve such an effect upon every listener that frequently not an eye remained dry, while many would break out into loud sobs, for there was something wonderful in his expression in addition to the beauty and originality of his ideas and his spirited style of rendering them.

The course of Beethoven's life was profoundly affected by deafness, whose first signs appeared a few years after his arrival in Vienna when he was in his mid-twenties. At first he tried to conceal his condition because, as he confessed in a will he drew up in 1802:

> It was not possible for me to say: speak louder, shout, because I am deaf. Alas, how would it be possible for me to admit a weakness of the one sense that should be perfect to a higher degree in me than in others, the one sense which I once possessed in the highest perfection, a perfection that few others of my profession have ever possessed.... For me there is no recreation in the society of others, no intelligent conversation, no mutual exchange of ideas. Only as much as is required by the most pressing needs can I venture into society. I am obliged to live like an outcast.

Beethoven's hearing continued to deteriorate and during the last decade of his life he was almost totally cut off from experiencing the performance of music. At the premiere of his great *Ninth Symphony* in 1824, he sat among the performers, following the manuscript of the score, but hearing nothing. As reported in a contemporary account:

> At the performance, a man went up to him at the end of each movement, tapped him on the shoulder and pointed to the audience. The motion of the clapping hands and the waving of handkerchiefs caused him to bow, which gave rise to great jubilation.

Beethoven's deafness brought his career as a pianist to a premature end. In his frustration at not being able to hear, he would strike the keys with such force that he broke hammers and strings, while in soft passages, he would play so lightly that no sound came out. He was also compelled to curtail his activities as a conductor because of incidents such as one where "the deaf composer caused the most complete confusion among the singers and orchestra and got everyone quite out of time, so that no one knew any longer where they went."

Beethoven's social relationships also suffered. Beethoven would speak, but the spontaneity of the conversation suffered because those with whom he spoke had to write down their words. Many of these conversation books have been preserved and are an important source of information about Beethoven's thoughts, personal relationships, and daily routine. Observers of the time frequently describe Beethoven as eccentric and coarse-mannered, and these qualities seem to have been accentuated by his deafness. For example, he spoke too loudly and often hummed to himself when out walking.

As Beethoven retreated more and more from the world, he directed his energies increasingly to composition, for though he could no longer hear with his physical ear, he experienced music and worked out his musical ideas in his hearing mind. According to his account:

> I carry my ideas about with me for a long time, often for a very long time, before I write them down. In doing so, my memory is so trustworthy that I am sure I will not forget, even after a period of years, a theme I have once committed to memory. I change a great deal, eliminate much, and begin again, until I am satisfied with the result. The working-out, in extension, in paring down, in height and in depth begins in my head and, since I know what I want, the basic idea never leaves me. It mounts and grows, I hear and see the work in my mind in its full proportions, as though already accomplished, and all that remains is the labor of writing it out.... You will ask me where I get my ideas. That I cannot say with certainty. They come unbidden, indirectly, directly. I could grasp them with my hands. In the midst of nature, in the woods, on walks, in the silence of the night, in the early morning, inspired by moods that translate themselves into words for the poet and into tones for me, that sound, surge, roar, until at last they stand before me as notes.

During the last years of his life, Beethoven was in poor health off and on. Early in the winter of 1826 he became progressively weaker and died in March of 1827. His funeral, three days after his death, was attended by 20,000 people.

Beethoven has long been recognized as one of the towering geniuses in music and as one of the great figures in artistic expression generally. Probably more than any other composer, his music suggests the grappling of a courageous soul with universal meanings and truths. The originality and profundity of many of his works, especially those from the last decade of his life, still astonish and challenge performers and listeners today. His compositions include 9 symphonies, 32 piano sonatas, 16 string quartets, and one opera as well as numerous other orchestral, chamber, piano, and vocal compositions.

Bernstein, Leonard (1918–1990)

The beginning of Leonard Bernstein's career as one of the 20th-century's most remarkable figures in the world of serious music is usually dated as 1943 when, at the age of 25, he was called to substitute for the indisposed conductor of the New York Philharmonic. At this time, Bernstein had studied composition and conducting at Harvard, the Curtis Institute of Music in Philadelphia, and the Berkshire Music Center in Massachusetts; he had become involved with a circle of popular entertainers who performed at the Village Vanguard in New York City; and he had been employed as an arranger and transcriber of popular songs and jazz. His conducting of the nationally broadcast concert of the New York Philharmonic was praised in rave reviews on the front page of the *New York Times* and in other newspapers. This critical acclaim thrust him into public spotlight, a position he was to retain for the rest of his life.

Over the next decades, Bernstein conducted many of the world's greatest orchestras, including the Boston Symphony, Vienna Philharmonic, Metropolitan Opera, and the New York Philharmonic, of which he served as the first American-born music director from 1958 to 1969. His warm personality, engaging public manner, and dynamic style at the podium drew large and devoted audiences to his concerts. Millions also learned about music, from standard repertory to experimental styles and jazz, through his radio broadcasts, televised lectures, young people's concerts with the New York Philharmonic, and from his books on music. He was a particularly effective spokesman for music by American composers, which he programmed frequently. Like John Kennedy, a friend with whom he shared liberal political views, Bernstein embodied a particular image of the American character through his energetic enthusiasm, engaging freshness, photogenic good looks, and ability to communicate with all kinds of people.

Bernstein's creative output was wide-ranging, from major concert-hall, chamber, vocal music and opera to scores for film, dance and Broadway musicals. He drew upon many musical styles, fusing elements from popular music and jazz with traditional art music practices. His own Jewish heritage finds voice in the thematic material of several important works, including the two symphonies subtitled *Jeremiah* and *Kaddish*. But he believed music was an international language and strove to transcend boundaries and reconcile differences through his work as a musician. In his own words, "I count the artist to be a citizen, a politic contributor to the art of living together in this lovely land and on this trembling planet."

Among Bernstein's best-known works are *Mass*, which was commissioned by Jacqueline Kennedy Onassis for the opening of the John F. Kennedy Center for the Performing Arts in Washington in 1971; the film score for *On the Waterfront*; the comic opera *Candide*; and the musicals *Wonderful Town* and *West Side Story*. The latter opened in 1957 at the Winter Garden Theater and was Bernstein's greatest Broadway success.

Cage, John (1912–1992)

John Cage was born in Los Angeles. By the time he was in his mid-twenties, he was at the forefront of experimental music both as a composer and as an exponent of new concepts in music. His originality as a thinker may be attributable in part to the fact that his father was an inventor. Cage was not the follower of any "school" of composition. Although he studied privately with Arnold Schoenberg and was a student in his music theory courses at UCLA, Cage's later music would transcend the total control implied by Schoenberg's serial techniques in favor of a music free of intention, memory, and personal likes and dislikes. Indeed, Cage's notions about the materials and experience of music were equally shaped by his study of Zen Buddhism and other Eastern philosophies as they were by his study of the compositional methods of Schoenberg and the music of Anton Webern. Contact with the music of non-Western cultures was also important in the formation of Cage's style. In the words of Henry Cowell, a pioneering American composer and theorist whose example profoundly influenced Cage, "the future progress for composers of the Western world must inevitably go toward the exploration and integration of elements drawn from more than one of the world's cultures."

Cage regarded all sounds, including noise, as legitimate materials for his compositions, so in addition to "normal" musical sounds he employed such untraditional sources as automobile brake drums, thunder sheets, and radios. While studying with Schoenberg, Cage worked in a book bindery and after hours started a percussion orchestra with his coworkers. Cage invented his own instruments for the group drawing on the waste materials found in and around the shop (scrap wood, metal objects, etc.). Years later, in Seattle, Cage was asked to compose percussion music for a dance, but only had a grand piano available to him. Remembering some of the piano pieces by Henry Cowell, Cage experimented with putting small objects between and around different strings of the piano, transforming its timbre so that it sounded like a percussion ensemble. This became one of Cage's best-known inventions, the **prepared piano**.

Silence can be as important as sound in a work of Cage. A prime example, inspired by the white paintings of Robert Rauschenberg, was *Four Minutes, Thirty-Three Seconds*, composed in 1952 and premiered that same year on August 29th in Woodstock, New York by the pianist David Tudor. In this performance Tudor came on stage, sat down at the piano, started a stopwatch, and closed the lid on the piano keyboard to begin the piece. He followed a musical score with a vertical line drawn on it showing the precise duration for each soundless event, turning the pages as time passed. After thirty-three seconds Tudor opened the keyboard lid and reset the stopwatch ending the first movement. For the second movement Tudor followed the same procedure of stopwatch and keyboard lid, ending after two minutes, forty seconds, and likewise for the third movement, which lasted one minute, twenty seconds.

Cage was, in effect, asking the audience to experience whatever aural events occurred during that period of time as being part of his composition, whether ambient sounds or silence. (In fact, one realizes very quickly that *Four Minutes, Thirty-Three Seconds* is anything but silent.)

Cage's goal was to let sounds exist purely for their own sake within the time structure that he had established. In his words, the composer should "set about discovering means to let sounds be themselves rather than vehicles for man-made theories or expressions of human sentiments." The Woodstock audience, a group of fellow artists and musicians normally sympathetic to the avant-garde, was perplexed by this piece and the first performance ended in a riot.

Four Minutes, Thirty-Three Seconds was the culmination of a search that began for Cage at the end of World War II when he saw what extreme human intention led to in Nazi Germany. He was "concerned about why one would write music at this time in this society?" It eventually became clear to him "that the function of art is not to communicate one's personal ideas or feelings, but rather to imitate nature in her manner of operation." Cage found in the *I Ching* (the Chinese Book of Changes), with its random procedure for obtaining an oracle numbered from one to sixty-four, an objective model of how nature operates. After 1950 Cage began to use the *I Ching* to determine the pitches, durations, and other essential aspects of his music; initially by using the coin oracle (tossing three copper coins six times) and later by programming a computer to generate a virtual coin oracle. The result was "chance music," in which significant aspects of composition and/or performance are governed through chance procedures, like the *I Ching*, in order to free the music from ego, memory, and taste. With *Four Minutes, Thirty-Three Seconds*, Cage used the *I Ching* to compose the piece "note by note," it just turned out that each note, according to the *I Ching*, was silent. His composition *Radio Music* is performed by tuning to chance (*I Ching*) determined stations on eight radios, producing a mixture of talk, music, and silence, depending on whatever is on the air at the moment.

Cage also experimented with giving performers greater freedom in their interpretation of his music. The instructions for one work read "for any number of players, any sounds or combinations of sounds produced by any means, with or without other activities" (which could include dance and theater). These experiments were not always successful. At the premiere of Cage's *Concert for Piano and Orchestra* he found that some of the musicians "introduced into their performance sounds of a nature not found in [his] notation characterized for the most part by their intention, which had become foolish and unprofessional."

The scores Cage composed as the music director of the Merce Cunningham Dance Company were conceived independently of the choreography, so in performance, music and dance simply coexist rather than being consciously shaped as a unified work. In addition to his long association with Cunningham, Cage was a close friend of the artists Robert Rauschenberg and Jasper Johns, both of whom depicted common objects in their paintings, for example, Johns' series of the American flag, or numbers and letters of the alphabet. In explaining this interest in everyday experience, Cage described his intention as "to affirm this life, not to bring order out of chaos nor to suggest improvements in creation, but simply to wake up to the very life we're living, which is so excellent once one gets one's mind and one's desires out of the way and lets it act of its own accord."

Chopin, Frederic (1810–1849)

Frederic Chopin was born near Warsaw, Poland, of a French father and a Polish mother. He was a precocious child but largely self-taught in music, receiving most of his formal training during his high school years at the Warsaw Conservatory. In 1829 he toured Germany and Italy as a pianist. On a second tour, which took him to France in 1831, he found Parisian life and society so congenial that he settled there for most of the remainder of his life. His extraordinary playing and personal charm won him many admirers among the aristocracy and in artistic circles. Among his artist friends was the novelist George Sand, the pen name of the novelist Aurore Dudevant, with whom he began a liaison in 1838. After their separation in 1847, tuberculosis, from which he had been suffering for many years, weakened his already frail constitution. He died in Paris.

Chopin's compositions are almost exclusively for the piano. Of the three major keyboard instruments (piano, harpsichord, organ), the piano is the most familiar and widely used today, and also the most recent. Its complete name is pianoforte, Italian for soft-loud, reflecting the fact that varying the pressure with which the keys are depressed directly influences the force of the hammers that strike the strings and thereby gives the player control over the volume of sound. The piano was invented in Italy in the early 18th century but did not attract serious attention from composers and performers until the time of Haydn and Mozart. At this early period it was a comparatively small, light-framed instrument of delicate tone. By the time of Chopin, at the height of the romantic period, its pitch and dynamic ranges had been expanded to essentially those of the modern piano.

During the 19th century, public concerts largely replaced aristocratic patronage as a major source of income for performers. Audiences of the time expected to be dazzled by the virtuosity of performers they went to hear and many of Chopin's works are technically very challenging. But despite his popularity and success as a concert artist, Chopin soon retired almost totally from public appearances, preferring to play for small groups of friends and admirers. As he observed about himself, "I am not the right person to give concerts. The public intimidates me. I feel asphyxiated by the breath of the people in the audience, paralyzed by their stares and dumb before that sea of unknown faces." Indeed, much of his music seems unsuited to a large concert hall setting. Contemporary observers refer to Chopin as a "tone poet" and typically stress the delicacy and sensitivity of both his music and his style of playing it. He was particularly known for his use of rubato, slight pushing forward and pulling back in tempo for expressive purposes. Even his flashiest, most virtuosic works, such as the concertos and etudes, require the performer to balance technical prowess with nuances of tempo, dynamics, and tone color.

Coltrane, John (1926–1967)

After Charlie Parker, saxophonist and composer John Coltrane is probably the most widely imitated saxophonist in jazz. Born the son of a minister in North Carolina, he was something of a late-bloomer as a musician; his earliest recordings, from the 1940s, show only a shadow of the genius he would become. But by the mid-1950s, he was one of the most important jazz musicians on the scene, and the recordings he made with Thelonious Monk and Miles Davis (especially Davis's *Kind of Blue* from 1959) are now legendary.

A gentle, deeply spiritual man, Coltrane was also obsessed with music: It was not uncommon for him to spend an entire night practicing in his room after playing three sets in a jazz club. His style showed immense authority of his instrument, yet also a deep passion gained from his early exposure to black church music and his experience playing with rhythm-and-blues bands in the 1940s. He is also noteworthy as a composer of such jazz standards as "Impressions," "Naima," and "Giant Steps," the latter—with its complex, rapidly changing chord structure—still a "test" piece for aspiring jazz musicians. Coltrane's quartet of the 1960s—which featured bassist Jimmy Garrison, pianist McCoy Tyner, and drummer Elvin Jones—was, along with Miles Davis's Quintet, one of the most important jazz ensembles of the decade. This group recorded, in 1964, what is widely considered Coltrane's masterpiece: the four-movement suite *A Love Supreme*. This work, inspired by a "religious awakening" Coltrane experienced in 1957, featured in its last movement the "sermonizing" on saxophone of a text Coltrane wrote himself, which is included with the liner notes. Coltrane also became deeply interested in avant-garde jazz of Ornette Colemen and others, recording in 1965 a 40-minute nearly atonal group improvisation called *Ascension*. Coltrane was strongly interested in Eastern spirituality and philosophy, and some even came to view him as something of a religious mystic (though he never encouraged this trend himself). To this day there is still a Church of St. John Coltrane in San Francisco, which features weekly performances of music from *A Love Supreme*. His early death from liver cancer, at age 40, was an immense loss to the jazz community.

Copland, Aaron (1900–1990)

Aaron Copland was born in Brooklyn of Russian Jewish immigrant parents. He was the last of five children and the only child who was not given music lessons. However, he picked up the rudiments of the piano from an older sister and then, on his own initiative, began formal piano lessons and later studies in harmony and counterpoint. He also attended concerts at the Brooklyn Academy of Music. At 20 Copland followed the path that had become traditional for young American artists: He set off for several years of study and travel in Europe. He returned to the United States in 1924, thoroughly trained in techniques of French modernism and strongly under the spell of Stravinsky, as evident in works composed at this time. But Copland had also become interested his own national heritage and shared with other American composers a desire to cultivate a style both modern and uniquely American. In his own words:

> We wanted to find a music that would speak of universal things in a vernacular of American speech rhythms. We wanted to write music on a level that left popular music far behind— music with a largeness of utterance wholly representative of the country that Whitman had envisaged.

He saw his goal as creating "a musical vernacular, which, as language, would cause no difficulties to my listeners" while at the same time "composing in an idiom that might be accessible only to cultivated listeners." The attempt to reconcile "low brow" and "high brow" has challenged many American composers of the last century and led to new syntheses such as rock opera and symphonic jazz.

Copland's American orientation is reflected in the subjects of many of his compositions, for example, the ballets *Billy the Kid* (1938), *Rodeo* (1942), and *Appalachian Spring* (1944); his scores for films based on stories by John Steinbeck, Thornton Wilder, and Henry James; and orchestral works with such titles as *John Henry, Lincoln Portrait,* and *Fanfare for the Common Man.* His quotation of folk tunes and use of jazz rhythms, his sturdy, wide-ranging melodies and energetic rhythms, and the openness and clarity of his orchestration are among the "American" features of his style.

At his death, Copland had become one of the most influential figures in American music. In addition to his composing activities, he was a leader in promoting new music through his books and articles, the concerts he organized and musician's groups he founded, his lectures at Harvard and The New School, and his teaching of young composers. His own creative work received crucial support through private patronage, prizes, and commissions. His many awards include a Pulitzer Prize, an Oscar, and the Presidential Medal of Freedom.

Davis, Miles (1926–1991)

Trumpeter, bandleader, and composer, Miles Davis was one of the most important jazz musicians of the post–WW II period. With a restless spirit and hugely creative imagination, he participated in (and often led) some of the most important developments in jazz after the early bebop records of the mid-1940s. Davis began his career playing on some of the important early bebop sessions, accompanied by musicians such as Charlie Parker. In the late 1940s he began a long collaboration with arranger and composer Gil Evans, which resulted in two of the most important and popular jazz albums ever produced: *The Birth of the Cool* (1949) and *Kind of Blue* (1959). The latter remains possibly the best-selling jazz album of all time. In these sessions, and many others, Davis reinterpreted the legacy of Charlie Parker and Dizzy Gillespie, softening the edges somewhat, and focusing on distinctive sonorities *(Birth of the Cool* featured a large ensemble that included a French horn). In the late 1950s, Davis explored "modal jazz"—that is, jazz improvisation that is built on a particular scale rather than a chord progression. In "Flamenco Sketches" from *Kind of Blue,* for example, the soloists are given five scales and allowed to improvise on each as long as they wish. Davis's influential quintet of the 1960s, which featured saxophonist Wayne Shorter, drummer Tony Williams, bassist Ron

Carter, and pianist Herbie Hancock, helped redefine the role of the rhythm section in jazz (making it an equal partner with the other soloists) and often featured loose improvisations on melodic motives and tonal centers, rather than chords. In the late 1960s, strongly influenced by rock and soul groups (especially Sly and the Family Stone), Davis made the controversial move to amplified instruments and rock-based rhythms, particularly in his album *Bitches Brew* (1970). He is considered at the forefront of the jazz-rock fusion movement, and many alumni from his group (including Shorter and Hancock) went on to play with highly successful fusion groups. In the 1980s, Davis continued to remain relevant by surrounding himself with younger musicians and recording current popular songs, such as "Human Nature," featured on Michael Jackson's *Thriller* album. In 2006, Davis was inducted posthumously into the Rock and Roll Hall of Fame.

Dvorak, Antonin (1841–1904)

The Czech composer Antonin Dvorak was one of Europe's most accomplished composers of the latter 19th century and one of the most influential figures of the nationalist movement in what is now Czechoslovakia. His romantic orchestral, choral, and chamber works were often influenced by Slovic and other Eastern European folk music.

In 1892 Dvorak accepted a position at the National Conservatory of Music in New York to teach composition and orchestration and to conduct the choir and orchestra. The following year Dvorak composed one of his most famous pieces, Symphony no. 9, *From the New World*, which was premiered in Carnegie Hall in December of 1893. Based on simple pentatonic themes, which Dvorak believed were common to Native American and African American folk music, the piece occasionally evokes a feeling of African American spirituals and includes a fragment from "Swing Low Sweet Chariots" in the G major theme of the work.

In 1893 Dvorak penned an article in the *New York Herald* in which he urged American composers to turn to their own folk music, particularly African American melodies and Native American chants, as source material for compositions that would reflect a distinctly "American" flavor. While a number of composers tried unsuccessfully to work with Native American materials, black spirituals influenced the works of a number of American composers including George Gershwin, Aaron Copland, William Grant Still, Harry Burleigh, and Duke Ellington.

Dylan, Bob (b. 1941)

Born Robert Zimmerman in Duluth, Minnesota, singer/songwriter/poet Bob Dylan is the most influential popular folk singer in the post–WW II years. After a year of college Dylan dropped out of the University of Minnesota and in early 1961 arrived in Greenwich Village where he became a rising star in the burgeoning folk music scene. His gruff voice and wailing harmonica on his first recording of traditional ballads, blues, and gospel songs made for Columbia Records in 1962 became his trademark. On his second album, *Freewheelin' Bob Dylan* (1963), he demonstrated his prowess as a brilliant songwriter with such pieces as "Blowing in the Wind" and "Don't Think Twice Its All Right." The former established Dylan as a national figure when the popular folk trio Peter Paul, and Mary made the song a hit in 1963. Over the next two years Dylan turned out a number of topical songs in the Woody Guthrie/Pete Seeger tradition. Pieces such as "Masters of War," "It's a Hard Rain Gonna Fall," "The Times They Are a Changing," "With God on Our Side," "Only a Pawn in Their Game," and "Oxford Town" were seething indictments of war and racism in America. These protest songs earned him the title of "the voice of the new generation," a role he would soon reject. As he matured, his lyrics began to become more abstract and surreal in songs like "Mr. Tambourine Man" and "My Back Pages."

In 1965 Dylan shocked the folk music world by appearing at the Newport Festival with a loud, raucous electric backup band. Accused of "selling out" the acoustic folk music revival with his electric rock-influenced arrangements, Dylan nonetheless went on to forge a new sound that critics dubbed "folk rock." In 1965 and 1966 he released three albums of original songs backed by an electric band that today are considered his most creative work. His overt protest songs had evolved into more subtle and poetic critiques of modern society and individual alienation with compositions such as "Maggie's Farm," "Subterranean Home Sick Blues," "Mr. Jones," "Desolation Row," and his anthem-like "Like a Rolling Stone," which charted number two in summer of 1965 and established Dylan as a bona fide rock star.

Following a motor cycle accident in 1966 Dylan became reclusive and did not tour again until the mid-1970s. He continued to write enduring songs that demonstrated his genius for transforming elements of traditional country, blues, and spiritual songs into fresh, modern-sounding compositions.

Ellington, Edward Kennedy "Duke" (1899–1974)

Ellington was born into a middle-class black Washington family. His father was a butler in the White House and had the means to provide his son with a solid education and cultural opportunities, including piano lessons. For a brief period after winning a high school poster designing contest, Ellington ran his own sign-making business. However, he soon gave up commercial art to play piano in Washington clubs, then in 1923 moved to New York where he became leader of a small combo. In the late 1920s his band began a five-year stint at the famous Cotton Club in Harlem, which established him as a pianist, composer, and arranger of genius and originality. Recordings and international tours over the next decades spread the reputation of Ellington's band and at his death in 1974 he was widely recognized as perhaps the most versatile and accomplished creative force in the history of jazz. His many honors include presidential medals, honorary degrees, and keys to many cities all over the world. He earned the nickname "Duke" early in life because of his personal refinement and elegance.

Among the sources of Ellington's music are the blues, the "hot" style of solo improvisation, and images of urban life ("Take the 'A' Train," "Harlem Air-Shaft"). His compositions have been estimated at six thousand, including popular songs, instrumental pieces, film scores, musical comedies, ballets, and an opera. He was the first jazz composer to enlarge the scope of jazz composition, extending the length of individual works and employing devices of thematic treatment associated with the Western classical tradition. In the last decade of his life he devoted himself especially to writing sacred music, a natural expression of his deep religious faith. Although he was an extraordinary pianist, Ellington generally gave himself only a modest role in his music, commenting that "my instrument is not the piano, it's the orchestra." Indeed, his compositions characteristically feature other members of his band. These included many of the best musicians of the time, and Ellington's arrangements and orchestrations were always heavily influenced by their personalities. As the membership of the band changed, so did Ellington's style so that many of his works have been recorded in quite different interpretations.

Gershwin, George (1898–1937)

The son of Russian Jewish immigrants, Brooklyn-born George Gershwin began his musical career as a Tin Pan Alley pianist and songwriter, quickly rising to prominence as a writer for the Broadway stage and composer of orchestral works. Gershwin began taking formal piano lessons at the age of twelve, and as a teenager worked as a house pianist in a musical publishing house in Midtown's legendary Tin Pan Alley. There he absorbed the sounds of musical theater, Broadway popular songs, and ragtime. His first hit song, "Swanee" (written in 1919 with lyrics by B. G. DeSylvia) sold over a million copies when popularized by the famous singer Al Jolson, and propelled Gershwin onto the Broadway Stage where he would write some of America's most notable musicals. His most successful shows, including *Lady, Be Good* (1924), *Oh Kay* (1926), *Funny Face* (1927), and *Girl Crazy* (1930), were written in collaboration with his lyricist brother Ira Gershwin (1896–1983) and featured songs heavily influenced by the syncopated rhythms and blues tonality of ragtime and early jazz. Gershwin's musicals helped define the modern American musical that moved beyond the vaudeville-derived review to a show with an integrated plot and sophisticated musical score.

Although he lacked formal conservatory training in music theory, composition, and orchestration, Gershwin nonetheless was determined to write serious music. In 1924 his first extended orchestral composition, *Rhapsody in Blue*, premiered in a concert of new works billed as "An Experiment in Modern Music." Gershwin's *Rhapsody* was built around five distinctive themes that reflected his genius as writer of memorable melodies, and incorporated syncopated rhythms, blues tonalities, and jazzy instrumental shadings (such as the use of muted brass). The success of *Rhapsody* and his subsequent compositions *Concerto in F* (1925) and *An American in Paris* (1928) established him as a leading figure in the emerging symphonic jazz movement that sought to create extended compositions by fusing European orchestral forms and instrumentation with jazz-inflected rhythms and tonalities.

Gershwin's achievements with symphonic jazz in the 1920s and the sophisticated operettas of the 1930s—*Strike Up the Band* (1930), *Of Thee I Sing* (1931, the first musical comedy to win the Pulitzer Prize), and *Let'm Eat Cake* (1933)—led critics of both decades to cast him as a contender for the honor of creating the first distinctly American opera. In 1935 he premiered *Porgy and Bess*, based on the 1926 novel *Porgy*— DuBose Heyward's wistful tale of life, love, and death in Catfish Row, a semi-fictitious black slum situated adjacent to the bustling docks of Charleston, South Carolina, the author's hometown. Part opera and part Broadway musical, *Porgy and Bess* remains one of America's most enduring staged works, and produced several of Gershwin's most memorable songs including "Summertime," "It Ain't Necessarily So," and "I Loves You Porgy."

In 1936 Gershwin relocated in Los Angeles and the following year wrote the soundtrack for the popular movie *Shall We Dance* staring Fred Astaire and Ginger Rogers. But that year Gershwin unexpectedly fell ill and died of a brain tumor at the age of 38. Today his songs, musicals, and opera endure and he remains one of America's most beloved songwriters and perhaps its most popular composer.

Gillespie, John Birks "Dizzy" (1917-1993)

Jazz trumpeter, pianist, arranger and composer. Along with Charlie "Yardbird" (or "Bird") Parker, Gillespie is credited as one of the founding fathers of modern jazz. He was originally self-taught on a variety of instruments, but in 1933 he attended the Laurinberg Institute in North Carolina. After two years playing trumpet with the school's band, he moved to Philadelphia, where he met trumpeter Charlie Shavers. It was through Shavers that Gillespie was introduced to the artistry of his great musical hero, trumpeter Roy Eldridge; in fact, many of his early solos are very much in Eldridge's style. It was in Philadelphia that Gillespie's clowning earned him the nickname "Dizzy" (sometimes shortened to "Diz."). Gillespie moved to New York in 1937, and joined singer Cab Calloway's band in 1939. It was in this band that the trumpeter met Afro-Cuban percussionist Mario Bauzá, sparking a lifelong interest in the fusion of jazz and Latin American music. Gillespie also provided some imaginative compositions and arrangements for Calloway's ensemble. Gillespie first met Parker in 1940, and was soon participating in the after-hours jam sessions that would give rise to the new jazz style known as "bebop." Gillespie made a variety of important recordings with Parker before the latter's premature death in 1955. He performed with some of the most important jazz artists of his day, and, with conga player Chano Pozo, made some of the earliest explorations into the fusion of jazz and Afro-Cuban music, the most famous being "Manteca" of 1947. In the 1950s, Gillespie toured internationally for the State Department. In the 1980s, he returned to work with small groups, often with younger musicians, and continued performing up to the time of his death. He usually played a peculiarly bent horn, which, though originally the result of accidental damage, produced a tone he preferred. It is now housed in the Smithsonian Institution.

Handel, George Frederic (1685–1759)

George Frederic Handel was born in Halle, a town in northern Germany where he received his early musical instruction from a local organist. In accordance with his father's wishes, he prepared for a career in law. On his father's death in 1703, Handel moved to Hamburg where his first two operas were successfully staged. In 1706 he accepted an invitation to Italy. The dramatic and Latin church music he composed during his three years in Florence, Rome, Naples, and Venice reveal the profound influence of his contacts with Italian musicians, particularly in his development of a richly expressive melodic style. In the words of one historian, "He arrived in Italy a gifted but crude composer with an uncertain command of form, and left it a polished and fully equipped artist." In 1709 Handel accepted a position in Hanover, Germany, but with the provision that he be granted a year's leave in London. He enjoyed considerable success with both the English nobility and public and in 1712 he returned to London, which became his home for the rest of his life.

Handel composed a phenomenal number of vocal and instrumental compositions, many of them intended for public performance for the rising English middle class. The pressures of continually producing new works led him to reuse his own material and to draw on that of others, generally without attribution. When asked about his borrowing from one particular composer, Handel is reported to have responded that the material in question was "much too good for him, he did not know what to do with it."

Handel was particularly drawn to composing operas on Italian librettos, which during the Baroque period favored stories from Greek mythology and ancient history. The plots provided a loose framework for extravagant display of vocal virtuosity that, along with lavish scenic effects, drew audiences to hear their favorite singers. Numerous contemporary accounts describe audiences talking, eating, and playing cards during the recitatives, waiting for their favorite singer's next aria. One of the bizarre manifestations of this superstar adulation was the castrati, male sopranos and altos whose change of voice had been surgically prevented during puberty. The practice, originally associated with the choir of the Sistine Chapel in Rome, continued into the 19th century and is said to have produced voices with the purity and range of a boy but the strength and endurance of a man. The career of one of the most famous castrati of Handel's day is the subject of the 1995 film, *Farinelli*. Leading male roles were assigned to the castrati, for example, the role of Caesar in Handel's *Guilio Cesare in Egitto* (Julius Caesar in Egypt). In contemporary revivals of Baroque operas, castrati roles are either sung by a woman or by a countertenor (a man with an alto range), or the music is transposed down to a normal male range.

Handel composed over 40 operas, most during his years as the musical director of London opera companies. In addition to providing new operas each season, either by himself or other composers, Handel made yearly trips to the continent to engage the sensational singers who the public would pay to hear. During intermission, audiences were treated to Handel performing his organ concertos.

Another important category of Handel's output is the oratorio, whose musical structure is similar to that of opera, but is based on a religious subject and performed without costumes, scenery, and acting. The Old Testament furnished the material for most of Handel's 25 oratorios—among them *Saul, Israel in Egypt, Samson, Joshua,* and *Solomon*—which were presented in public concert halls during Lent, when operas and other theatrical entertainments were banned from the stage. The texts of the oratorios are in English, which probably contributed to their enormous popularity with the English public. His instrumental works include concertos, the *Water Music* performed for King George I by musicians on a barge in the Thames, and *Music for the Royal Fireworks* for a fireworks display.

Hardin (Armstrong), Lillian (1898–1971)

Lillian Hardin, a pianist and composer, was one of the few women to forge a long and successful career in the male-dominated world of early jazz and in a segregated America. Born in Memphis, Tennessee, she took piano lessons as a child and briefly attended Fisk University before moving with her family to Chicago in 1917. Because she could read music, she got a job demonstrating sheet music at a music store, where she attracted the attention of local bandleaders. While performing with King Oliver's Creole Jazz Band, she met Louis Armstrong. They married in 1924 and Hardin (Armstrong) is generally credited with encouraging the young trumpeter to strike out on his own. During the 1920s she played the piano and sang on many of the recordings of the Hot Five and Hot Seven and composed several of the group's hit songs. Though usually relegated to the role of accompanist, her occasional solos show a talented pianist strongly influenced by Jelly Roll Morton (whom she knew well), and even hint at a well-developed classical technique. During the 1930s Hardin (Armstrong) worked in New York, where she appeared in several Broadway shows and also led her own swing band. She returned to Chicago in 1940 where she continued to perform in nightclubs and record. Armstrong and Hardin separated in 1931 and were divorced in 1938, but they remained friends for the rest of their lives. In August of 1971, while playing in a memorial concert for Armstrong who had died the previous month, Hardin (Armstrong) suffered a massive heart attack and died.

Haydn, Franz Joseph (1732–1809)

The details of Haydn's early life are sketchy. He was born in an Austrian village and came from a humble background. At about the age of eight he was chosen to join the choir of one of Vienna's most important cathedrals. After his voice changed, he supported himself by teaching and working as a freelance performer, then at the age of 29, entered the service of a wealthy and powerful Hungarian aristocratic family, the Esterhazys. Music was a central component of life at the Esterhazy estate in the Hungarian countryside and the household staff included orchestral musicians, opera singers, and a chapel choir. Haydn's contract specified that he was responsible to provide music as required by the prince, care for the musicians and instruments, and conduct himself "as befits an honest house officer in a princely court." For 30 years Haydn lived and worked at the Esterhazy palace, largely isolated from what was happening elsewhere. As he himself recalled, "My prince was content with all my works, I received approval, I could, as head of an orchestra, make experiments, observe what created an impression, and what weakened it, thus improving, adding to, cutting away, and running risks. I was set apart from the world, there was nobody in my vicinity to confuse and annoy me in my course, and so I had to become original." With the succession of a new Esterhazy prince in 1790, Haydn's life took a new direction. Although he continued to earn a salary, he was no longer required to live at the Esterhazy estate. He moved back to Vienna, one of the musical capitals of the time, where he met and befriended Mozart and for several years was the teacher of the young Beethoven. He also accepted invitations for two lengthy trips to London, for which he composed a number of important new works. In London, performances devoted to his music, including 12 brilliant new symphonies, were highlights of the concert season. He appeared before the royal family, was sought after as a guest at social occasions, and was awarded an honorary doctorate from Oxford University. In Vienna, where his monumental oratorios *The Creation* and *The Seasons* were enthusiastically received, he was named an honorary citizen. At his death at the age of 77, Haydn had become one of Europe's most celebrated figures.

Haydn's vast compositional output includes 52 piano sonatas, 104 symphonies, concertos for a variety of instruments, works for a variety of chamber groupings, masses and other sacred vocal music, operas, and oratorios. Written over more than a half century, his works document the transition from the late Baroque to the mature classical style, to which he himself made definitive contributions. In his works in sonata form, he deepened and extended practices of motivic development and he elevated the string quartet from one of many possible groupings to the most important chamber music ensemble. His late symphonies balance simplicity of themes with brilliant orchestration. And his musical language encompasses a broad spectrum of expressive content—folk-like innocence, intense passion, playfulness, high-spirited humor, tenderness, joyful exuberance, sorrow.

Ives, Charles (1874–1954)

Charles Ives was born in New England. He received a thorough education, including college at Yale where he studied composition and was organist of a New Haven church, in addition to pursuing a regular academic program. But the most profound influences on his personality and political, religious, and aesthetic views were his New England heritage and his father, a village bandmaster and something of a renegade in his musical thinking. After graduation from Yale, Ives came to New York where he began a successful career in the insurance business, believing that "a man could keep his music interest stronger, cleaner, bigger and freer if he didn't try to make a living out of it." He composed evenings and weekends, completing hundreds of songs, choral works, piano pieces, and works for a variety of instrumental groupings, from a few players to a full symphony orchestra. The strain of this rigorous routine took its toll and in 1918 Ives suffered his first heart attack, after which he gradually retired to a life of seclusion with his wife, Harmony, at their home in Connecticut. At his death his works, most of which were in manuscript, were just beginning to attract attention outside the small group that had long recognized his originality and importance as a truly American voice.

Ives's music, with its bold, adventurous experiments with tonal materials and structures, is rooted in the American ideals of rugged independence and freedom of individual expression, which also inspired such observations as the following:

"Beauty in music is too often confused with something that lets the ears lie back in an easy chair."

"Down with politicians & Up with the People!"

"Some of these… pieces…were in part made to strengthen the ear muscles, the mind muscles, and perhaps the Soul muscles, too."

"The great fundamental truths—freedom over slavery; the natural over the artificial; the goodness of man; the Godness of man; God."

Many of Ives's works are highly personal recreations of his own experiences, memories, and imagination with such titles as *George Washington's Birthday*, *Central Park in the Dark*, *The Circus Band*, *From the Steeples and the Mountains*, *Harvest Home Chorales*, *The Concord Sonata*, *General William Booth Enters into Heaven*. The titles of others—*Three Quarter-Tone Pieces for Two Pianos*, *Chromatimelodtune*, *Tone Roads*, for example—suggest the abstract, purely musical dimension of Ives's compositional thinking. In both types, he often quotes or imitates marches, ragtime, patriotic, folk, and popular songs within a complex, dissonant, and seemingly discontinuous musical fabric.

Joplin, Scott (1868–1917)

Joplin was born and raised in Texarkana, on the border between Texas and Arkansas. His father, an ex-slave, scraped together enough money to buy a piano for his musically inclined son, who soon taught himself to play with remarkable facility. In his early teens Joplin left home to seek a musical career in St. Louis, Chicago, and Sedalia, Missouri, finally moving to New York in 1907. Joplin's compositions include about 50 rags for piano, a folk ballet, and two operas. Though the earliest of his operas, *A Guest of Honor*, has been lost, the second, *Treemonisha*, was completed in 1910 and though never fully staged at the time has since become a staple of the operatic repertoire. His early piano rags, especially "Maple Leaf

Rag" of 1899, brought him considerable fame and fortune and earned him the title King of Ragtime. But with the passing of the ragtime craze after the first decade of the new century, and the increasing complexity of his compositions, Joplin found little appreciation for his work. Afflicted by syphilis, Joplin's health declined until his death in 1917.

Josquin des Prez (c. 1440–1521)

One of the greatest composers of the Renaissance, Josquin des Prez was born in the north of France and spent about two decades of his creative career in Italy. His first appearance in documents as a musician comes in 1477, when he is named as a singer in the court of Rene of Anjou in France. The early 1480s are largely unaccounted for, but by the middle of the decade he was working for Cardinal Ascanio Sforza of Milan, before moving to work for the papal chapel in Rome. After a period of employment at the Florentine court of Duke Ercole d'Este in the early 1500s, he returned to France where he died.

Although biographical detail about Josquin is scant, including the exact date and place of his birth, there is ample evidence of his fame during his own day. Aristocratic patrons vied to have him in their employ, even passing over highly respected contemporaries who were known to be cheaper, easier to get along with, and more reliable about completing work on time. He was particularly admired for his mastery of counterpoint and his gift for expressing the meaning of words in his musical settings, an important goal of humanist composers. In the words of one commentator, "Josquin may be said to have been, in music, a prodigy of nature, just as our Michelangelo Buonarroti has been in architecture, painting and sculpture. Thus far there has not been anybody who in his compositions approaches Josquin. As with Michelangelo, among those who have been active in these his arts, he is still alone and without a peer. Both have opened the eyes of all those who delight in these arts or are to delight in them in the future." One surviving portrait thought to be of Josquin is attributed to Leonardo da Vinci, and his death was mourned in several musical laments.

The invention of music printing during Josquin's lifetime, coupled with his fame and popularity, ensured the preservation of a large number of his works and his enduring reputation today. Recent scholarship indicates some works formerly attributed to Josquin were, in fact, by other composers but published under Josquin's name to ensure wider sales. As reported by one commentator toward the end of the period, "I recall that a certain famous man said that Josquin wrote more compositions after his death than during his life."

Josquin's surviving output is entirely vocal and, even discounting disputed works, impressive in quantity: 18 complete setting of the Mass, over 100 polyphonic settings of Latin religious texts (motets), and about 80 on French and Italian secular texts. Most are for four voices—soprano, alto, tenor, bass—and, following the practice of the time, to be performed a cappella, that is, by voices alone, without instruments. His gracefully shaped vocal lines interact in a highly contrapuntal web, diverging, converging, crossing, echoing, and imitating each other, sometimes with great rhythmic independence, sometimes in hymn-style texture.

King, B. B. (b. 1925)

Riley B. King, better known as B. B. King, is unquestionably the most influential bluesmen of the 20th century. Born on a plantation near Indianola, Mississippi, he moved to Memphis in the late 1940s where he gained local fame as a singer, guitarist, and host of a weekly blues show on WDIA, the first major radio station to go to an all black format in 1948. His 1951 R& B hit "Three O'Clock in the Morning" launched a recording and touring career that would eventually make him the world's most renowned blues singer.

King's guitar style, based around eloquent single-string runs, is a refinement of techniques pioneered by legendary blues guitarists Blind Lemon Jefferson, Robert Johnson, and T-bone Walker. King's guitar solos were backed by smooth, riffing horns and a pulsing rhythm section that combined to define a style know as "jump blues" in the 1950s. His early vocals were in the vein of classic blues shouters, but as he matured his voice took on a distinctive gospel feel, characterized by a soulful, pleading delivery complete with falsetto swoops, shouts, and extended melismas (stretching a single syllable over several pitches).

In the late 1960s, following appearances at the Newport Folk Festival and Bill Graham's legendary rock palace the Filmore West, King extended his popularity among younger white audiences. Eric Clapton, George Harrison, and the Rolling Stones were among the many rock stars who idolized King's music and who recognized his contributions to the development of rock and roll. In the new millennium King's sophisticated blues sound continues to move black and white audiences, and his Time Square blues club (opened in 2000) remains a center of blues activity in New York City.

Charles Mingus (1922–1979)

Jazz composer, bassist, and band leader Charles Mingus is one of the most creative proponents of modern jazz. Born in Arizona in 1922, he grew up in the Watts section of Los Angeles, where in school he studied trombone, cello, and bass, learning both jazz and classical techniques. He toured with big bands led by Louis Armstrong and Lionel Hampton before moving to New York in the early 1950s. There he worked with bop musicians Charlie Parker, Dizzy Gillespie, and Bud Powell before staring his own ensemble in the mid-1950s. During this period he became active in New York's Jazz Composer's Workshop, and eventually abandoned written transcription and began dictating his compositions to his players by ear, allowing them considerable room for personal interpretation. By the early 1960s he had established himself as the premiere bassist in jazz, and a leading composer for both big band and small ensemble formats.

Mingus drew on many styles, ranging from blues, gospel, and big-band swing to bebop and modern jazz that featured dissonant, collective improvisation. Among his best know compositions are the bluesy *Haitian Fight Song* (1957), the extended jazz suite *Pithecanthropus Erectus* (1956) that chronicles the rise and decline of modern civilization with a finale of cacophonous improvisation, and the classical sounding *Half-mast Inhibition* (1960). Mingus objected to categories like "classical" and "jazz," choosing rather to construct extended works that combined compositional forms, themes, and complex harmonic changes associated with classical music with techniques of individual and group improvisation, complex rhythms, and tonal elements of blues and gospel common to jazz.

Perhaps the most important jazz composer of the mid 20th century, Mingus summed up his creative philosophy on liner notes to the 1956 *Pithecanthropus Erectus* LP:

> I "write" compositions—but only on mental score paper—then I lay out the composition part by part to the musicians. I play them the "framework" on piano so that they are all familiar with my interpretation and feeling and with the scale and chord progressions to be used. Each man's own particular style is taken into consideration, both in ensembles and in solos....In this way, I find it possible to keep my own compositional flavor in the pieces and yet to allow the musicians more individual freedom in the creation of their group lines and solos.

Monk, Meredith (b. 1942)

One of America's foremost experimental composers, Meredith Monk grew up in New York City in an artistic household. Her mother was a professional singer, working primarily in radio through the nineteen-thirties and forties. Although Monk identifies herself as a composer, she does not separate music from the other performing arts. While a student at Sarah Lawrence College she studied singing, composition, and dance and performed in theater as a student in their combined performing arts program. Her earliest works, such as *16 Millimeter Earrings*, included film along with music, theater and dance, establishing Monk as a significant multidisciplinary artist and eluding classification of her work by critics until the term *performance artist* came into usage.

Monk is less interested in telling a narrative story through her performance art than she is in creating an experience where all of the faculties are employed. The music, words, movement, and staging all have equal importance. She is an attentive listener to the sounds in her environment and she often develops *extended performance techniques* in order to replicate some of those that are more interesting. The influences on her extended vocal techniques, in particular, include the music of non-European cultures (harmonic singing and ululation), city sounds (the glissando of a car alarm), and the sounds of nature (bird song and animal cries).

In *Dolmen Music*, Monk allows us to peak into an archaic community inspired by her reaction to seeing the dolmen in Brittany (*La Roche aux Fées*). Her initial response to *The Fairy Rocks* inspired her to infuse the work with the sense of being ancient and futuristic at the same time. A Meredith Monk piece usually has no specific interpretation yet many works, like *Memory Song* and *Gotham Lullaby*, are so intimate that they often engender an explicit meaning in the listener based on their life experiences.

While the timbres that Monk creates may be complex and unusual, the music underlying her work is often simple and consonant. The pure open intervals of medieval music are especially attractive to Monk. She once stated that the European music that she most admired began with the Medieval and went through to the Renaissance, skipped the Common Practice Period, and continued with 20th/21st Century music. One of her favorite composers is Perotin.

Monk, Thelonious (1917–1982)

Pianist and composer. Monk is one of the most important figures in jazz history, but he is also one of the most controversial and least-understood. Born in Weehawken, New Jersey, Monk's family moved to New York when he was four, and he remained there the rest of his life. In the early 1940s he became house pianist at Minton's in Harlem, helping to formulate what would become "bebop"—the style that would define modern jazz—though Monk himself never considered himself a "bebopper" and his music does not fit easily into that category. Monk was a highly accomplished pianist, but his idiosyncratic keyboard technique—full of dry, punchy chords, complex syncopations, intentional "wrong notes," and long stretches of silence—led many to believe mistakenly that he was simply a poor musician. His erratic personal behavior did little to improve his stature in many peoples' eyes, though his influence on other musicians such as Dizzy Gillespie and John Coltrane remains legendary. Monk's most important contribution to jazz may be as a composer, for pieces such as "Round Midnight," "Straight No Chaser," and "Ruby, My Dear" not only became jazz standards but expanded harmonic, rhythmic, and formal possibilities for those who improvised on them. Recent scholarship—much of it as yet unpublished—will hopefully provide a better understanding of this enigmatic musician.

Mozart, Wolfgang Amadeus (1756–1791)

Wolfgang Amadeus Mozart was born in Salzburg, an Austrian cathedral town where his father was a violinist in the orchestra of the archbishop, an important official in the Roman Catholic Church. All evidence indicates that Mozart's natural musical gifts were phenomenal and became apparent at an early age. When he was six, his father took him on the first of several extended European tours, one lasting more than three years, during which he astonished audiences with his ability to compose, improvise, and perform at the keyboard and on the violin. The many surviving letters between members of the Mozart family and friends back home in Salzburg record the highs and lows of these trips, from the exhilaration of command performances before royalty to the dangers and discomforts of travel by coach and several serious illnesses that afflicted Mozart and his older sister, Nannerl, including typhoid fever. Herr Mozart's reference to Wolfgang cutting a tooth reminds us that these trips began when he was the age of a first grader of today.

After his experiences in London, Paris, Rome, Venice, Amsterdam, and other musical capitals of the time, Salzburg seemed provincial and confining. But when at the age of 17 he had not been offered a satisfactory position in any large city, Mozart grudgingly entered the service of the archbishop. He found his duties in Salzburg abhorrent and his treatment by the archbishop demeaning. Frequent disagreements ensued, culminating in a stormy encounter in 1781 during which the archbishop released him from service "with a kick on my behind," as Mozart reported in a letter.

Mozart spent the rest of his life in Vienna, the capital of the Hapsburg Empire, home of the Empress Maria Theresa and Emperor Joseph II, and one of Europe's major cultural centers. Although he held some minor court appointments, he was one of the first composers to seek a career as a free agent rather than in the employ of the church or aristocracy. For a few years he presented a series of very popular and lucrative concerts of his own works, among them 12 spectacular piano concertos in which he was featured as the soloist. He also received several commissions to compose operas, among them *Marriage of Figaro* and *Don Giovanni*, which premiered in Prague in1786 and 1787, respectively. But Mozart's success was sporadic and short-lived. He died at age 35 and was buried in a common grave, his impoverished circumstances due in part to his extravagant tastes and inability to manage his finances. In retrospect he also emerges as a tragic casualty of a society in transition, a man too proud and conscious of his own genius to abase himself in the service of the ruling class, yet too profound a musical thinker to be appreciated by the new bourgeois audience.

Mozart was an extraordinarily prolific composer, creating enduring works in virtually every genre of his day—operas, symphonies, piano sonatas, chamber music, works for the Roman Catholic Church. As a composer of the classical period, the ideals of clarity and balance inform Mozart's music, from his early piano pieces written at age six and seven through his great opera *The Magic Flute* and the unfinished *Requiem Mass* from the last year of his life. What sets him apart from his contemporaries is the mastery of counterpoint, intensity of developmental processes, expressive power, and sophisticated orchestration that characterize works written during Mozart's decade in Vienna. This maturing and deepening of his compositional craft, while also creating works that would be accessible, seems to have been a conscious pursuit. As he wrote to his father in 1782:

> These concertos are a happy medium between what is too easy and too difficult. They are very brilliant, pleasing to the ear, and natural, without being vapid. There are passages here and there from which connoisseurs alone can derive satisfaction; but these passages are written in such a way that the less learned cannot fail to be pleased, though without knowing why.

Two hundred and fifty years after his birth, Mozart's works remain staples of the concert repertory of artists and ensembles all over the world.

Parker, Charlie "Yardbird" or "Bird" (1920–1955)

Though his life was brief and often tragic (he died at the same age as Mozart), Parker made a profound impact on jazz that is still felt today. In fact, Parker and Louis Armstrong are probably the most significant and influential figures in all of jazz history. Born in Kansas City, Missouri, he started playing alto saxophone at age 13, and played around his hometown for several years until taking a brief trip to New York in 1939. From 1940 to 1942, he toured with Jay McShann's band and made several recordings. He also participated in informal jam sessions at Minton's in Harlem and other New York jazz clubs, helping to create the music that would become known as "bebop." In 1945 he participated in some important recording sessions with fellow bebop musician trumpeter Dizzy Gillespie. His most influential and productive years were from 1947 to 1951, when he performed extensively and made dozens of recordings that have become indispensable jazz classics. Plagued by years of drug and alcohol abuse, Parker died just a week after his final performance at Birdland, a club named in his honor. As a composer of many tunes that have become jazz standards, Parker's harmonic inventiveness and rhythmic sophistication have influenced legions of jazz musicians. His nickname, according to McShann, came from an incident while on tour, when the band's bus hit a chicken (or "yardbird") that Parker insisted on having cooked up by their host. But the moniker, especially in its shorter form "Bird," seemed to fit Parker and his flights of musical brilliance perfectly.

Piazzolla, Astor (1921-1992)

Piazzolla was world-famous as a composer, bandleader, and virtuoso of the *bandoneón*, a type of 38-key accordion considered one of the crucial instruments of the traditional tango ensemble. A child prodigy, Piazzolla was born in Argentina, but his family emigrated to the US in 1924. Thirteen years later they returned to their homeland, where Piazzolla made arrangements for some of Argentina's most popular bandleaders and studied classical music with the great Argentine composer Alberto Ginastera. In 1944 Piazzolla formed his own band, which featured primarily his own compositions. In 1954 he went to Paris to study with legendary teacher Nadia Boulanger, who felt his tango compositions showed great promise. He returned to Argentina, and for the next twenty years worked with his own tango groups. In 1974 he returned to Paris. Piazzolla's distinctive music became known as *nuevo tango* ("new tango") and was at first widely criticized by those who felt he had abandoned some of the important traits of the nearly century-old tango tradition. However, he was later widely viewed as responsible for tango's renewed international popularity, as the music's audience had declined sharply in the 1950s and 60s. In the 1980s, his works were featured by important classical performance groups, including the Kronos Quartet. At the time of his death he was at work on an opera about the life of Carlos Gardel, a hugely popular tango singer of the 1920s and 30s. He composed about 750 works, including a symphony, a concerto for *bandoneón*, and a sonata for the great Russian cellist Mstislav Rostropovich.

Presley, Elvis (1935–1977)

Known around the world as "the King of Rock and Roll," Elvis Aaron Presley was born in Tupelo, Mississippi, the son of a poor white truck driver. Presley and his family moved to Memphis in 1948, where he was exposed to both white country and black R&B and gospel music. In 1954, the year after he graduated high school, he made his first recordings at Sam Philip's now legendary Sun Studios on Union Avenue in Memphis. Philips had recorded both white country singers and black blues singes, but in Presley he discovered a young white man who had exceptional feel for the black music, as demonstrated on his early blues covers "That's All Right Mama" (original by Arthur Crudup), "Good Rockin' Tonight" (original by Roy Brown), and "Mystery Train" (original by Jr. Parker). Accompanied by the twangy electric guitar of Scotty Moore and bouncing bass of Bill Black, Presley's sound was dubbed "rockabilly" by early critics in deference to his hillbilly roots and his ability to rock the blues.

Presley appeared on the Grand Ole Opry and the Louisiana Hayride live radio shows, but it was not until Philips sold his contract to the major record label RCA that Presley would become a teen idol and national star. In 1956 and 1957 he recorded over a dozen hit songs, with "All Shook Up," "Hound Dog," "Teddy Bear," "Jailhouse Rock," and "Don't be Cruel" charting number one on the pop, country, and R&B charts. His appearances on the popular TV shows Milton Berle, Steve Allen, and Ed Sullivan shows brought him further fame and earned him the title "Elvis the Pelvis" due to his sexually suggestive dancing. In 1958 Elvis entered the army, and after completing a two-year commitment returned to the United States to continue to record and pursue a career in the Hollywood. He died in his Memphis home in Graceland in 1977, the victim of drug abuse.

Presley's early Sun and RCA recordings are considered by many critics to be the pioneering sounds of rock and roll. Presley was the first white pop singer to popularize black rhythm and blues, and in doing so he opened the door for innumerable young white artists to become rock and roll singers. His success demonstrated the tremendous allure black R&B held for the baby boomer generation, and the willingness for white musicians to embrace and at times exploit black music.

Puccini, Giacomo (1858–1924)

Giacomo Puccini was born in Lucca, Italy, into a family whose members had been prominent musicians, mostly church organists, for several generations. He was not a child prodigy and his early musical studies gave little promise that he would fulfill his mother's ambition that he follow in the family tradition. The turning point was apparently attending a performance of Verdi's *Aida* when he was 18, after which he decided to devote himself to opera. For three years, 1880 to 1883, he studied seriously at the Milan Conservatory, but his early works were failures with audiences and critics and have not remained in the repertory. His third opera, *Manon Lescaut* of 1893, was a triumph and demonstrated the extraordinary sense of theater that was to characterize the six other full-length and three one-act operas he completed over the course of his life.

Puccini was drawn to stories of passionate relationships set in exotic locations. His reputation rests largely on three operas: *La Boheme* (1896) that takes place around 1830 in the Latin Quarter of Paris, *Tosca* (1900) in several historic sites in Rome, and *Madame Butterfly* (1904) on a hillside overlooking Nagasaki, Japan. Puccini's last opera, *Turandot*, is set during a legendary time in Peking (Beijing), China. Puccini, a chain smoker, developed throat cancer and died while he was working on the final scene, which was completed by another composer. At its premiere in 1926 in Milan, at the point in the score where Puccini had stopped working, the conductor, Arturo Toscanini, stopped the performance, turned to the audience and said, "Here the opera finishes, because at this point the Maestro died."

The power of Puccini's scores lies in his gift for writing music that evokes and intensifies the passions and atmosphere of each dramatic situation. A particularly effective device is recalling music associated with earlier moments in the story, but now heard in the new context of the evolving drama. His poetic imagination is also apparent in lush harmonic language and sensuous orchestration. Expressive melody is continuous, either sung in soaring arias that climax at the top of the singer's range or shifted to the orchestra during passages of vocal recitative. Puccini roles require singers with tremendous vocal strength, technical virtuosity, and emotional projection.

Reich, Steve (b. 1936)

Steve Reich was born in New York City. His early musical studies were lessons on piano and percussion. He graduated with honors in philosophy from Cornell University in 1957 and subsequently studied composition at The Juilliard School in Manhattan and at Mills College in California. While on the West Coast, he developed an interest in electronic music, jazz, African drumming, and the Balinese gamelan, the percussion ensemble of Bali and other Indonesian islands. In 1966 he founded the New York–based ensemble, Steve Reich and Musicians, devoted exclusively to the performance of his own music. In the 1970s, he studied drumming with a master drummer of the Ewe tribe at the Institute of African Studies in Ghana, and Balinese gamelan music at the Center for World Music in Berkeley, California. More recently he has pursued an interest in traditional forms of cantillation of the Hebrew Scriptures.

Reich first became known as a leading exponent of musical minimalism, a movement of the 1970s that grew out of a predilection for extreme simplification in painting and sculpture in the 1960s. Minimalism was to some extent a reaction against serialism and other complex and highly intellectual theories of composition. In developing compositional techniques and formulating an aesthetic for their new musical language, minimalist composers looked to popular music and non-Western cultures, in Reich's case, to Africa and the islands of Indonesia. In his own words, "I studied Balinese and African music because I love them and also because I believe that non-Western music is presently the single most important source of new ideas for Western composers and musicians." While in Ghana, he was introduced to a structural concept of the "timeline," a basic rhythm over which other musicians play repeated rhythmic patterns, with the most complex performed by the group leader or master drummer. The essential organization is thus polyrhythmic, the simultaneous performance of independent repeated patterns resulting in a complex interplay of rhythmic layers.

The materials of minimalist composers are short melodic, rhythmic, and harmonic patterns. Reich's musical materials may be originally composed, or samples from recorded speech and urban sounds. A taped phrase of a street vendor, for example, supplies the main musical idea of *Check it out,* one of the five movements of *City Life.*

Whether original or borrowed, patterns are repeated and gradually transformed over musical spans ranging from a few minutes to a half hour or more. Through a technique called phasing, a pattern gradually moves out of sync with itself, becoming its own counterpoint. The rate of change in minimalist music is slow, creating a hypnotic effect that reflects the influence of Eastern mysticism and practices of meditation embraced by Reich and other minimalist composers.

Schoenberg, Arnold (1874–1951)

Arnold Schoenberg was born in Vienna. He did not come from a musical family and was largely self-taught in music, learning the violin and cello without benefit of study with a good teacher. His formal education ended when financial circumstances following the death of his father forced him to take a job as a bank clerk, but he continued to pursue his interests in literature, philosophy, and music on his own. Schoenberg was drawn to the ferment that characterized artistic and intellectual movements around the turn of the century and allied himself with the Viennese avant-garde. His first compositions are clearly indebted to late romantic influences, but a more personal style, characterized by extreme chromaticism and polyphonic complexity, emerged in an outpouring of works written in his thirties. Between 1915 and 1923, Schoenberg stopped composing, devoting himself to the formulation of his twelve-tone theory of composition on which all of his works after 1923 are based. In 1925 he was appointed a professor of composition at the Berlin Academy of Arts, which provided a supportive environment for experimental art. This situation changed radically when Hitler came to power in 1933. Schoenberg, vulnerable to persecution as an artist and because of his Jewish background, emigrated with his family from Germany, landing first in Great Brittan and eventually immigrating to the United States. He taught at the University of California at Los Angeles until his retirement in 1944, and continued to compose until his death.

Since medieval times, Western music theory had been based on the concept of a key center, or tonic, in melodies and harmonies, and on the distinction between consonance and dissonance in the relationship between voices in music of two or more parts. These are seminal principles that form the underpinnings of the religious music of the Renaissance, the fugues and cantatas of Bach, the symphonies of Beethoven, the operas of Mozart and Verdi, and other masterpieces of Western art music. At the end of the 19th century, however, there was a sense among progressive musicians that the major/minor system and the compositional procedures and forms it had produced had run their course. It was in this atmosphere of searching for alternative approaches that Schoenberg came up with a new theory of composition. Perhaps his lack of formal training in a discipline where complex problems of form, counterpoint and harmony, instrumentation, and notation have traditionally required years of study with a master freed him to think outside established conventions. In any case, Schoenberg's "method of composing with twelve tones" was a radical departure from traditional compositional procedures. Central to the method is his revolutionary idea that all twelve tones into which the octave is divided in Western music should be treated as equal. In other words, no tone would dominate as a tonic. The composition of a work according to Schoenberg's method begins with the creation of a tone row containing all twelve pitches. This row is the germinal cell from which all melodic, harmonic, and contrapuntal materials are derived. The principles for configuring a tone row and the complex ways it can be manipulated are formulated in Schoenberg's theoretical writings. Because of the absence of a key center, twelve-tone music is often called "atonal," a term to which Schoenberg objected, or "serial" because the compositional technique involves manipulation of a tone row, or series.

While twelve-tone describes Schoenberg's compositional procedure, his style is classified as expressionist. Expressionism was an early 20th-century movement that sought to reveal through art the irrational, subconscious reality and repressed primordial impulses postulated and analyzed in the writings of Freud. Rather than depict impressions received from the outer world, painters such as Wassily Kandinsky, Oskar Kokoschka, Edvard Munch, and Max Beckmann, and writers such as August Strindberg, Frank Wedekind, Stefan George, and Franz Kafka explored the shadowy and distorted images, hallucinatory visions, and irrational terrors of the subconscious. Hysteria, isolation and alienation, the grotesque and macabre were favorite subjects of Expressionist artists. Schoenberg himself took up painting in 1908 and, over the course of his life, created imaginatively intense if technically amateurish pictures, including several self-portraits. In the music of Schoenberg and other Expressionist composers, relentless emotional intensity is attributable to jagged, highly disjunct melodic lines; instruments in extreme ranges; unresolved tension through avoidance of consonant sonorities; texts dealing with violence and abnormal behavior; and exaggeration and distortion of the natural accents of speech.

Schoenberg applied the twelve-tone technique to every type of genre to which he contributed—opera; choral and solo vocal; orchestral, chamber and keyboard. His music, never readily accessible or easy to listen to, has always aroused controversy, even hostility, on both aesthetic and intellectual grounds. He was drawn to subjects and forms of expression that resonated with a devoted, if small, following, and he never sought to entertain or gain popularity with a wide public. In his own words:

There are relatively few people who are capable of understanding, purely musically, what music has to say. Such trained listeners have probably never been very numerous, but that does not prevent the artist from creating only for them. Great art presupposes the alert mind of the educated listener.

Schubert, Franz (1797–1828)

Franz Schubert received his earliest musical education from his father, a schoolmaster in a village outside Vienna, followed by formal study at a music school in Vienna and composition lessons with the composer Antonio Salieri (depicted as Mozart's rival in the play and movie *Amadeus*). For a brief period he taught at his father's school, but from the age of 18 to his death at 31, he was plagued by illness and poverty. Except for a few published piano pieces and songs for which he was miserably paid, his works had been heard by only a small group of friends and admirers and his genius was almost totally unrecognized for some time. Schubert produced a phenomenal number of works, from symphonies, operas, and church music to chamber works, piano pieces, and songs written for performance in the homes of the growing middle class. As he observed about himself, "I write all day and when I have finished one piece, I begin another."

Schubert was particularly successful in small, intimate forms, notably his piano pieces with such titles as *Moment Musicale* (musical moment) and impromptu, and his songs. He is considered to be the father of the art song, a composition for voice and instrumental accompaniment (most often piano) that flowered during the Romantic period. Unlike folk songs, which are passed on through oral tradition and usually of unknown authorship, art songs are notated (written down) songs in which a composer consciously seeks to develop expressive connections between poetry and music. The lyric poetry of Goethe, Schiller, and Heine in the late 18th century provided a rich source of texts for the outpouring of German art song in the 19th century. The concept of the art song was not Schubert's invention, but his over 600 songs demonstrate a facility for penetrating to the essence of a poem and forcefully enhancing its meaning and images that was unprecedented. He responded immediately and intuitively to poetry, often writing a song from start to finish in an afternoon. There is a story of friends leaving a poem lying out on a table for the unsuspecting to Schubert to happen upon, and returning a few hours later to discover it transformed into a completed song.

Schumann, Clara Wieck (1819-1896)

Clara Wieck Schumann is one of a small number of women prior to the second half of the 20th century whose musical activities included composition, a reflection of the relatively subordinate role women composers have played in the history of concert hall music. That their creative output has been less than that of men with respect to both quantity and quality is attributable to a number of factors, chiefly attitudes regarding women's appropriate role in society, presumptions about their inherent intellectual and emotional capacities, their lack of access of education and training, their financial dependence on men, and the exclusion of women from many forms of musical activity. The following assessment appeared in an 1891 article in Women's Journal:

> It is probably true that more women than men have received musical instruction of a sort, but not of the sort which qualifies anyone to become a composer. Girls are as a rule taught music superficially, simply as an accomplishment. To enable them to play and sing agreeably is the whole object of their music lessons. It is exceedingly rare that a girl's father cares to have her taught the underlying laws of harmony or the principles of musical composition.

> In Germany and Italy, the countries where the greatest musical composers have originated, the standard of women's education is especially low and the idea of woman's sphere particularly restricted. The German or Italian girl who should confess an ambition to become a composer would be regarded by her friends as out of her sphere, if not out of her mind.

> When women have had for several centuries the same advantages of liberty, education, and social encouragement in the use of their brains that men have, it will be right to argue their mental inferiority if they have not produced their fair share of geniuses. But it is hardly reasonable to expect women during a few years of liberty and half education to produce at once specimens of genius equal to the choicest men of all the ages.

Unlike most women of her day, Clara Wieck Schumann was carefully trained from the age of five as a pianist and musician by her father, Friedrick Wieck. In other areas, including the so-called feminine arts of sewing, knitting, or crocheting, her education was meager. She made her public debut in 1828, at age nine; the same year she met Robert Schumann, her future husband, who was then eighteen. Robert was to become one of the leading composers associated with musical romanticism. Between 1828 and 1838 Clara launched a highly promising career, and her friendship with Robert deepened into love. Her father vehemently opposed their relationship and, hoping to reassert his control, sent 19-year-old Clara to Paris with a total stranger as a chaperone. To his astonishment, and probably her own as well, she dismissed the chaperone and managed to support herself in the strange city. She presented herself to the French public through successful concerts she arranged, and she found students, composed music, and had her works published. Even today we would find this remarkable, but in 1839 it was an amazing act of courage, especially for a woman.

Schumann was considered the foremost woman pianist of her day and a peer of contemporary male virtuosi. Her concert programs and her high musical standards changed the character of the solo piano recital in the 19th century. She introduced much new music by her husband, and by Chopin and Brahms, and she was also distinguished as being the first pianist to perform many of Beethoven's sonatas in public. At the end of her long career, she had played over 1,300 public programs in England and Europe. Clara's training in composition was also excellent. Her compositions were published, performed and reviewed favorably during her lifetime, and she was encouraged by both her father and her husband.

Clara's marriage to Robert Schumann took place the day before her twenty-first birthday in 1840, after a lawsuit the couple brought against Wieck was decided in their favor. Both before and after her marriage, she wrote chiefly piano works and songs, genres considered appropriate for female creative expression since such works were intended primarily for performance in the home. Her output was also small, undoubtedly because of her hectic performing schedule and domestic responsibilities associated with raising eight children. With the exception of one work, Clara ceased composing after her husband's death in 1856.

Much of what is known about Clara's personal life after her marriage is found in her diaries, in her joint diaries with Robert, and in her letters. It is clear that, while she felt confident of her powers as a performer, she had ambivalent feelings toward her ability and skill as a composer. Comments such as the following from her 1839 diary reflect the prevailing notion of the time that women were unfit by nature for intellectual pursuits and limited to manners of expression which were inherently feminine in character.

> I once thought I possessed creative talent, but have given up this idea. A woman must not desire to compose – not one has been able to do it, and why should I expect to? It would be arrogance, although indeed, my father led me into it in earlier days.

Clara never intended to give up her concert career after her marriage, and Robert never seriously suggested it. Despite his desire for a quiet home and a woman to look after him and their children, he was aware of his wife's needs as an artist and his attitude toward her career was, for a man of his time, unusually enlightened and supportive. Clara's letters and diary entries indicate she recognized her importance as a pianist and considered herself first an artist and only afterward a parent. The conflicts between public concertizing and raising a family intensified in 1854 when Robert, suffering from mental illness and depression, entered a sanitarium where he died two years later. Clara was pregnant at the time he became terminally ill, and soon after the birth of their eighth child, she set out on the first of many concert tours that were to become a regular feature of her life for more than 30 years. She now bore the entire responsibility of providing for a large family. But she also seems to have felt a need for artistic self-expression, which she sought in performing. She may also have found comfort in bringing her husband's music to the attention of the public. As she wrote to a friend:

> You regard them [the concert tours] merely as a means of earning money. I do not. I feel I have a mission to reproduce beautiful works, Robert's above all, as long as I have the strength to do so, and even if I were not absolutely compelled to do so I should go on touring, though not in such a strenuous way as I often have to now. The practice of my art is definitely an important part of my being. It is the very air I breathe.

Seeger, Pete (b. 1919)

New York City–born Pete Seeger is undoubtedly the most well-known and influential figure of the mid-20th century urban folk song revival. The son of the erudite musicologist Charles Seeger and a professional violinist Constance de Clyver Edison, Seeger was educated at elite New England boarding schools before entering Harvard University where he joined John Fitzgerald Kennedy as a member of the class of 1940. But two years later he dropped out of college and moved to New York City in hopes of pursuing a career in journalism.

Seeger had begun playing the four-string banjo in a high school Dixieland jazz combo, but his interests shifted toward folk music after attending the Asheville, North Carolina folk festival in 1936 with his father. Charles, who was beginning to study and promote folk music through his position with the federal Resettlement Administration, introduced Pete to the famous folk music collector Alan Lomax, who offered him a temporary position working at the Library of Congress Archive of American Folk Music. There Seeger immersed himself in recordings of traditional Anglo and Afro American folk music and began teaching himself to play the guitar and five-string banjo.

Seeger relocated in New York City in the early 1940s where he sang with Woody Guthrie and Huddie "Lead Belly" Ledbetter in the burgeoning urban folk music revival. He helped found the Almanac singers in 1941, a loosely knit group of left-leaning folk singers and political activists who sought to use folk music to promote union and other progressive causes. In the 1950s he organized the Weavers, a more professional sounding folk ensemble whose 1950 recording of the Lead Belly song "Goodnight Irene" brought folk music to the popular music charts. Throughout the 1950s and early 1960s Seeger's solo concerts and recordings for Folkways Records put urban American audiences in touch with the rich heritage of traditional American ballads, blues, work songs, and spirituals. Seeger encouraged thousands of young people to pick up guitars and banjos and to discover American folk music. He also demonstrated that new folk songs could be written using traditional forms and instruments, as he authored or coauthored well-known anthems of the folk revival including "We Shall Overcome," "If I Had a Hammer," "Turn, Turn, Turn," and "Where Have all the Flowers Gone."

Seeger was devoted to using folk music to promote progressive political causes. His socialist leaning made him a victim of McCarthy blacklisting in the 1950s, and in the 1960s he emerged as a prominent voice in the civil rights, anti-war, and environmental movements. Today, in his late eighties, Pete Seeger remains an outspoken critic and controversial figure, beloved to old leftists and young progressives who see him as the "voice of the people," and reviled by conservatives who dismiss him and other urban folk singers as hypocritical leftist phonies.

Seeger, Ruth Crawford (1901–1953)

Composer and folk music transcriber Ruth Crawford was born in East Liverpool, Ohio. She studied piano as a child in Florida, and in 1921 moved to Chicago to study at the American Conservatory of Music. In Chicago, she became a friend of the poet Carl Sandburg and taught piano to his three daughters. Her work in arranging folk songs began with her association with Sandburg, to whose collection *The American Songbag* (1927) she contributed several exceptional piano arrangements.

Crawford's compositions impressed the composer Henry Cowell who generously assisted her professional career. He recommended her as a pupil to his friend Charles Seeger, a noted pedagogue, theorist, and philosopher of music, published several of her compositions in his influential *New Music Quarterly*, and helped her obtain a Guggenheim Foundation Fellowship. Crawford moved to New York in 1929, and became a vital participant in the "ultra-modern" school of composition, a group of composers that included Aaron Copland, Henry Cowell, Marc Blitzstein, and Earl Robinson. Through her studies with Seeger, Crawford became increasingly interested in linear writing and "dissonant counterpoint," a 20th-century approach to counterpoint that turned traditional contrapuntal rules on their head. Her best-known work is the *String Quartet 1931*, a striking example of modernist musical experimentation, which established her brilliant and inventive musical mind.

Crawford and Seeger married in 1932, and their first child, Michael, was born in 1933. After the birth of Peggy, their first daughter, in 1935, the Seeger family moved to Washington, DC, so that Charles could begin a position as a music specialist with the federal government's recently created Resettlement Administration. With four children in all (Mike, Peggy, Barbara, and Penny) to raise and a demanding schedule of teaching piano, Crawford stopped composing ultra-modern music, and turned to the work of teaching music to children and of collecting, transcribing, arranging, and publishing folk songs. Her three volumes of children's folk songs—*American Folk Songs for Children* (1948), *Animal Folk Songs for Children* (1950), and *American Folk Songs for Christmas* (1953)—helped introduce a generation of young Americans to folk music and fueled the urban folk revival of the late 1950s and early 1960s. Her son Mike, daughter Peggy, and stepson Pete would be major figures in that movement.

Shankar, Ravi (b. 1920)

Music from the Indian subcontinent is one of the non-Western repertories that has fascinated Western musicians and audiences in recent decades. One of its principal exponents has been the great sitarist Ravi Shankar. As a child he exhibited unusual gifts as both a dancer and a musician, but during his mid-teens began to focus on mastering the sitar. For years he studied as the discipline of a prominent guru, ultimately receiving the blessing of his teacher. His first tour outside India was to the Soviet Union in 1954. During the 1960s he became well known to Western audiences through his many tours and recordings. He has often performed for humanitarian causes, such as the 1958 UNESCO concert in Paris, the United Nations Human Rights Day concert in New York in 1967, and fund-raising events for Bangladesh. The 1971 "Concert for Bangladesh" with the Beatle George Harrison is available on CD and DVD. Harrison studied with Shankar, and their friendship led to Shankar's appearances at the Monterey Pop and Woodstock festivals.

Shankar is an undisputed master of the purest classical style of Indian music. He is also a composer and teacher. In his writings on music, he refers frequently to the spiritual dimension of Indian music, a system that "can be traced back nearly two thousand years to its origin in the Vedic hymns of the Hindu temples, the fundamental source of all Indian music. Thus, as in Western music, the roots of Indian classical music are religious. To us, music can be a spiritual discipline on the path to self-realisation, for we follow the traditional teaching that sound is God—Nada Brahma. By this process individual consciousness can be elevated to the realm of awareness where the revelation of the true meaning of the universe—its eternal and unchanging essence—can be joyfully experienced. Our ragas are the vehicles by which the essence can be perceived." He describes the experience of performing as one in which he infuses the "breath of life into a raga" and "each note pulses with life and the raga becomes vibrant and incandescent."

Shankar has also crossed the boundaries of traditional Indian music. The experimental side of his career is illustrated by his appearances with George Harrison of the Beatles and three recordings from the early 1970s—one of classical North Indian music with American violinist Yedudi Menuhin, another with Japanese musicians, and a third his Concerto for Sitar and Orchestra. Shankar has composed works for All-India Radio's instrumental ensemble and scores for ballets and films, including *Gandhi* and the *Apu Trilogy*. Shankar has exerted formative influence on Western musicians speaking a broad range of musical dialects, from the minimalist composer Philip Glass to pop groups such as the Beatles, Rolling Stones, and Traffic. His honors include membership in the American Academy of Arts and Letters and of the United Nations International Rostrum of Composers. His discography totals almost 70 albums and he currently holds the Guinness record for the longest international career in music. In recent years, Shankar has toured and recorded with his daughter, Anoushka, who also plays sitar. Another daughter is the pop musician Norah Jones.

Smith, Bessie (1894-1937)

Smith was born in Chattanooga, Tennessee. By the age of 14 she had become the protégé of the blues singer Ma Rainey and began performing in minstrel shows, cabarets, and vaudeville. Her tours and recordings during the 1920s brought blues to a wide audience and made her the best-known black artist of her day—the "Empress of the Blues." Her vocal style, which has been immortalized in 160 recorded selections, is characterized by expressive alterations of melody and rhythm, slurred intonation, blue-note inflections, and raspy, growling tone-color effects. She performed with many of the jazz greats, including Benny Goodman, Louis Armstrong, and James P. Johnson. Her commercial popularity declined along with that of the blues in the early 1930s. She died following a car accident near Clarksdale, Mississippi.

Stravinsky, Igor (1882–1971)

Igor Stravinsky, probably the most influential European-born composer of the 20th century, was born outside Leningrad. His father was a bass singer at the Russian Imperial Opera, but Stravinsky was encouraged to pursue a career as a government lawyer, studying music on an amateur level. However, with the encouragement of his teachers, when he was 20 he began to study composition seriously. By the time he was 30, two brilliant and audacious works, *The Fire Bird* and *Petrushka,* had thrust him into the forefront of the modernist movement. Both were ballet scores commissioned by Sergei Diaghilev, director of one of the most important ballet companies of the early 20th century, the Paris-based Ballet Russe (Russian Ballet).

From 1911 to 1939, Stravinsky resided principally in France and Switzerland, touring Europe as a pianist and conductor of his own works. His third collaboration with Diaghilev, *The Rite of Spring (Le Sacre de Printemps),* provoked a near riot at its premiere in 1913. The choice of subject, a pagan ritual in which a virgin is sacrificed to propitiate the gods, reflects a fascination with "primitive" or preliterate cultures that also inspired Picasso's collection of African sculpture and influenced the development of the Cubist style in art. This was also the period of Freud's writings about the fundamentally savage impulses of human nature. The raw sensuality and hypnotic musical repetition, paralleled by compulsively repeated choreographic movements, were among the features found offensive by members of the audience. One critic expressed the opinion that the work "constituted a blasphemous attempt to destroy music as an art." Others characterized it as "stupifying," "haunting," "a beautiful nightmare." Almost a century after its composition, *Rite of Spring* no longer stirs such impassioned controversy but continues to arrest listeners with the elemental power of the musical materials and the overwhelming force of their expression. One section of *Fantasia,* the pioneering 1940 animated film from the Disney Studios, is based on the score of *TheRite of Spring.*

In 1939, at the outbreak of World War II, Stravinsky was presenting a series of lectures at Harvard. Rather than return to Europe, he decided to settle in the United States, where he remained until his death. Over his long life, he completed a huge body of work encompassing virtually every musical genre—opera, ballet, symphony, concerto, choral, chamber. T. S.Eliot, Charlie Chaplin, and Pablo Picasso, who sketched a famous portrait of Stravinsky while sitting at a Paris café, were among his friends. He collaborated with many leading artists of his time, including Vaslav Nijinsky, George Balanchine, Jean Cocteau, Andre Gide, and W. H. Auden. He had an affair with Coco Chanel, gave autographs to Sinatra and the pope, and was honored at a White House dinner given by the Kennedys (whom he called "nice kids").

Like Pablo Picasso, Stravinsky went through different stylistic periods during which his works reflect a variety of past and contemporary traditions, most importantly the folk and classical music of his native Russia, the compositional practices of Bach and Mozart, jazz, and the serial technique of Arnold Schoenberg. Stravinsky seems to have been conscious of how seminal such influences had been on his evolution as a composer. When in 1969 he was asked to explain why, at age 87, he was moving from Los Angeles to New York, he replied, "to mutate faster."

Varèse, Edgard (1883–1965)

Edgard Varèse was born in Paris. His initial training was in math and engineering, but in 1903, over the objections of his family, he began serious musical studies in Paris and Berlin. None of his works from this period survive, although by 1915, when he moved to New York, he had acquired notoriety as a boldly original composer and thinker. In New York, Varèse became a leading advocate for new music, organizing concerts and founding the International Composers' Guild, the New Symphony Orchestra, and the Pan American Association of Composers. He considered the United States to be a place "symbolic of discoveries—new worlds on earth, in the sky, or in the minds of men."

Varèse was fascinated by the timbral aspect of music. In a 1915 interview he stated: "I refuse to submit myself only to sounds that have already been heard. What I am looking for are new technical mediums which can lend themselves to every expression of thought and can keep up with thought." He defined music as "organized sound" and asserted "the right to make music with any and all sounds," even those considered to be "noise." He often tried to persuade scientists and technicians to help him invent new instruments, and actively sought funding for such research.

Varèse's compositional output was small—twelve completed works and a handful of unfinished projects. But no two works are alike, each representing a unique solution in his search for ways to achieve the "liberation of sound." For example, *Ionisation* (1931) is scored entirely for percussion instruments, which until the early 20th century were used primarily in orchestral music for rhythmic emphasis and dramatic or coloristic effects, such as cymbal crashes. In addition to a huge array of traditional orchestral percussion, Varèse's score calls for instruments of non-Western origin as well as chains, sirens, and anvils. The piece unfolds as a succession of contrasting blocks and masses of sound. The title "ionization" suggests a connection between the interaction of electronically charged atoms or groups of atoms studied in physics and Varèse's concept of music as "moving bodies of sound in space." For his *Poeme Electronique,* Varèse recorded bells, sirens, the human voice, and other sounds which he manipulated electronically, created other sounds in a studio, and assembled them onto an 8-minute tape that played inside a futuristic building designed by the architect Le Corbusier for the Philips Pavilion at the 1958 Brussels Worlds Fair.

Verdi, Giuseppe (1813–1901)

Giuseppe Verdi was born in a village near Parma that, like the rest of northern Italy, was under Austrian control. His musical experiences up through his mid-twenties occurred close to home—early lessons with a local musician, church organist job at age 9, further private study after being denied admission to the Conservatory at Milan, a job giving instrumental and vocal lessons. A turning point in his life occurred in 1939 with the enthusiastic reception of his first opera, *Oberto*, in Milan. This led to a commission for three more operas, one of which, *Nabucco*, was produced in several major European cities and in New York in the 1840s. Once an obscure provincial musician, Verdi had achieved the international celebrity that he was to enjoy for the rest of his life, almost exclusively for his operas. Although openly critical of the Roman Catholic Church, he also composed several settings of religious texts.

Verdi's career coincides almost exactly with the Risorgimento, the nationalist movement that he passionately supported and that culminated with the unification of Italy under King Victor Emmanuele in 1861. Although the scenes and characters in Verdi's operas have no direct connection to contemporary events in Italy, the stories of tyranny, conspiracy, political assassination, and suppression of individual and national liberties struck a chord with the Italian public. The slogan of the unification movement became VIVA, VERDI, the letters of the composer's name standing for *Vittorio Emanuele, Re di Italia* (Victor Emmanuele, King of Italy). Toward the end of Verdi's life, opera was developing in new directions under the influence of German and younger Italian composers, but he was still beloved by his countrymen. The route of his burial procession in Milan was said to have been lined by as many as 200,000 people and an estimated 300,000 attended the official memorial service.

Almost 20 of Verdi's operas are staples of the romantic repertory today, among them *Macbeth, Rigoletto, Il Trovatore, La Traviata, Un Ballo in Maschera, La Forza del Destino, Don Carlos, Aida* and, from late in his life, *Otello* and *Falstaff*. With the exception of his first and last operas, which are comic, Verdi was drawn to passionate, eventful stories that are dark, violent, and end with the death of one or more major characters. In his words, "I want subjects that are novel, big, beautiful, varied and bold—as bold as can be." The librettos of three are based on Shakespeare, others on Friedrich Schiller, Voltaire, and the romantic writers Victor Hugo, Lord Byron, and Dumas. Having chosen his subject, Verdi worked closely with his librettists to construct fast-moving, eventful plots with vividly contrasting emotions. Conflicts between fear, love, jealousy, fidelity, patriotism create dramatic tension both between and within individual characters. As the libretto evolved, so did Verdi's ideas for the powerful melodies, energetic rhythms, and climactic buildups through which those passions would find musical expression. In casting his operas, Verdi looked for singers who brought to their roles a combination of high level of vocal accomplishment and vivid stage presence, qualities that continue to be the hallmarks of the great interpreters of Verdi today. In the words of the soprano Renata Tebaldi: "Verdi suffered a great deal through his life and I hear it in his music as the expression of his own soul. Singers must remember to try and achieve the greatest 'expressione' in singing Verdi to do justice to this great Maestro."

Vivaldi, Antonio (1678–1741)

Antonio Vivaldi was one of the most prolific and influential composers of the Italian Baroque. He received his musical education from his father, then at the age of 15 began his training for the priesthood. In 1703, the year of his ordination , he assumed the position of teacher of violin at the Pietá, a Venetian home for orphaned, illegitimate, and indigent girls. He spent most of the rest of his life in Venice, although productions of his operas took him to Rome, Mantua, Verona, and Prague. At the height of his popularity, his commissions and published works amassed him considerable wealth, but at the time of his death, in Vienna, he had become impoverished and was buried in a pauper's grave.

The list of Vivaldi's compositions is both large and diverse, encompassing orchestral and instrumental chamber works, masses and other sacred music, and operas. Of his over 40 operas, more than half have been lost and none are part of the standard operatic repertory today. On the other hand, his concertos, of which over 500 have been preserved, are firmly established in the instrumental literature. His music has been featured in numerous television commercials and in the scores of such recent films as *The Royal Tenenbaums, Sidewalks of New York, Being John Malkovich, The Talented Mr. Ripley, Final Cut,* and *Shine*.

Many of Vivaldi's concertos were written to be played by the more talented of his students at the Pietá. During one six-year period, from 1723 to 1729, the records of the Pietá show he was paid for 140 concertos, an astonishing twelve per month. These and other of his instrumental and sacred works would have been performed by the girls at concerts that became major events in the social life of the Venetian nobility and foreign visitors.

Vivaldi was a seminal figure in the history of the concerto, especially the violin concerto. About 200 of his 500 extant concertos are for one violin and another 30 or so for two or more violins, or violins with other solo instruments. His writing for the violin explores the instrument's virtuoso capabilities as well as its capacity to "sing." He standardized a three-movement design for the concerto as a whole, in which the fast tempo and animated character of the first and third contrast with a more lyrical and expressive slow movement in the middle. Vivaldi also established a formal pattern for the fast movements, called ritornello form, which involves a systematic alternation of solo and tutti forces. He was a pioneer of program music, instrumental music that portrays a story, scene, or other nonmusical subject. The most famous of his programmatic works is *The Four Seasons,* a collection of four violin concertos, one devoted to each of the four seasons of the year.

APPENDIX 2: GLOSSARY

Note: italicized words are Glossary entries.

Absolute music: instrumental music whose materials and structure have been conceived without influence from or reference to text, stories, pictures, or other nonmusical sources or meanings. *Sonata, concerto, symphony*, and string quartet are among the common titles assigned by composers to such works. Compare *program music*.

Accent: emphasis of a note or chord, often through dynamic stress, that is marked increase in loudness.

Accompaniment: the musical background for a principal part or parts. A musical texture consisting of melody and accompaniment is classified as *homophonic*. See Chapter 1: Elements of Sound and Music.

Aria: a number for solo voice and orchestra most commonly associated with *opera* and *oratorio*. Arias are vehicles through which characters tell us about themselves and express their feelings and emotions. The text of an aria is often poetic and is set to a highly developed melody. Words and phrases may be repeated. The orchestra accompanies, but instruments may also function as wordless characters that counterpoint and converse with the voice.

Art song: notated (written down) musical setting of a text authored by a known composer who consciously seeks to develop expressive connections between poetry and music. By contrast, *folk songs* are usually transmitted by oral tradition and their creators are unknown.

Beat: the regular pulse underlying the unfolding of music in time. The rate at which the beat occurs is called *tempo*. See Chapter 1: Elements of Sound and Music.

Blue notes: steps in the *scale*, usually the third and seventh, that are flattened, that is, slightly lowered in pitch, in performing blues.

Blues: see Chapter 6: American Vernacular Music.

Brass instrument: see Chapter 2: Musical Instruments and Ensembles.

Bridge: a section that connects two *themes*, often bringing about a *modulation*, as in *sonata form*. See Chapter 1: Elements of Sound and Music.

Cadence: the termination of a musical statement, analogous to a point of punctuation in prose. A complete or full cadence is characterized by the finality of a period or exclamation point at the end of an independent clause while the need for completion of a dependent clause, denoted by a comma or semicolon in prose, is the musical equivalent of an incomplete or half cadence.

Cadenza: passage near the end of an *aria* or *concerto* movement performed by the soloist without the *orchestra*. The material of the cadenza is intended to show off the virtuosity of the soloist and in some periods was improvised.

Call and response: in jazz, gospel, and other music influenced by African practices, alternation between two performing entities, most commonly a single performer and a group. See Chapter 6: American Vernacular Music and Chapter 7: Jazz.

Cantata: from the Italian *"cantare"* to sing, a genre of vocal music based on either a secular or religious text set as *recitatives* and *arias*, and sometimes *choruses*. Cantatas may have dramatic qualities but are unstaged and are much shorter than *operas* and *oratorios*.

Chamber music: see Chapter 2: Musical Instruments and Ensembles.

Chance music: an approach to creating a unique musical work in which the composer intentionally relinquishes control over pitches, durations, and other essential musical elements. The performer(s) determines what will be played and how it will be played by such means as tossing dice or coins.

Chant: *monophonic* setting of a sacred text. Chanting by a soloist or a choir in unison is practiced in many religious traditions, including Judaism, Christianity, Islam, and Buddhism. The intoning of sacred texts provides a manner of delivery that is differentiated from ordinary speech and can heighten the mystery and spiritual atmosphere of religious ritual.

Choir: a choral ensemble, especially one that performs religious music, as in a church choir or a gospel choir. When applied to instruments, choir is usually synonymous with "section," as in woodwind choir, brass choir.

Chord: three or more pitches sounding together that produce *harmony*.

Chorus: when referring to performers, a chorus is a vocal ensemble. Choruses vary greatly in size, from chamber-like groups of eight to twelve to a hundred or more singers. The performance of choral music most commonly requires sopranos, altos, tenors, and basses (see Chapter 2: Musical Instruments and Ensembles, section on Human Voice as Instrument) but there is also important choral literature for women, men, children, and boys. The other use of the word chorus denotes a section of a musical work, either the refrain of a song or, in a jazz composition, the harmonic/melodic theme and its varied repetitions.

Coda: from the Latin for "tail," a concluding section added to customary components of a musical form.

Common practice period: the time in European art music between 1600 and 1900 when composers spoke, and audiences understood, a common musical language based on tonality (keys) and standard instrumental forms. The Baroque period began this era with refinements to the tonal system still in progress, in the Classical period tonal music and instrumental forms (such as sonata form) reached their highest level of development, and in the Romantic period these systems broke down as composers began to sacrifice formal purity in exchange for personal expression in their music.

Concerto: an orchestral work in which the players are divided into two groups, one consisting of one or more *soloists*, the other being the full *orchestra* (called the tutti, meaning all the players). The term concerto derives from an Italian word that means both to join together in a cooperative manner and also to contend competitively. Much of the effect of the concerto derives from the virtuosity of the soloist and from contrasts of dynamics, mass of sound, and *tone color* made possible by the division into differently constituted groups.

Conjunct, disjunct: see Chapter 1: Elements of Sound and Music.

Consonance, dissonance: simultaneous pitches that are experienced as pleasing or harmonious within a particular musical context are described as consonant while those experienced as harsh or clashing are described as dissonant.

Continuo: in Baroque music, both the bass line that provides the harmonic foundation and the instruments that perform it. At least two players are generally required for the performance the continuo part: a cellist for the written-out bass line, and a harpsichordist or organist who plays the bass line with the left hand and improvises harmonies with the right hand. The continuo section is somewhat analogous to the *rhythm section* in jazz.

Counterpoint: principles and rules used in composing multi-part music; adjective, contrapuntal.

Development: in a general sense, the manipulation of musical material through such procedures as altering the melodic and rhythmic contours of a *theme*, stating *motives* derived from a theme in imitation or repeated at different pitch levels, stating the theme in different *keys*, and so on. In a more restricted sense, the section in a *sonata form* where musical ideas from the *exposition* are manipulated and elaborated.

Dissonance: see *Consonance*.

Downbeat: the first beat in a metric grouping, or measure. Patterns of arm motion used by the conductor signal the downbeat by a downward movement of the arm.

Dynamics: degrees of loud and soft. Commonly used Italian terms are *forte* (loud), *piano* (soft), *crescendo* (getting gradually louder), and *decrescendo* (getting gradually softer). See Chapter 1: Elements of Sound and Music.

Ensemble: from the French for "together," a group that performs together. Examples include an *orchestra*, band, *opera*, and *chorus* as well as groups with ensemble in their title, such as jazz ensemble, brass ensemble, and new music ensemble. In opera, an ensemble involves three or more soloists simultaneously singing different words and melodies, each conveying his or her view of a particular dramatic situation. See Chapter 2: Musical Instruments and Ensembles.

Episode: a passage between statements of a *theme* or subject, as in a *fugue* or *rondo*.

Ethnomusicology: from the Greek *"ethno"* (culture, people), the scientific study of music of oral tradition, encompassing tribal and folk music, and of the art music produced by various world cultures. The discipline, whose origins date back to the 1880s, draws on methodologies of musicology, the scholarly study of Western art music, and anthropology, whose subject is mankind and human culture.

Exposition: the section of a work in which the principal thematic material is presented. See *fugue* and *sonata form*.

Experimental music: music where the outcome is unknown until the piece is realized. Although the term did not exist when Charles Ives was active as a composer, due to his several musical innovations he is seen today as the father of American experimental music. Important experimental composers include Henry Cowell, John Cage, Cornelius Cardew, Annea Lockwood, Meredith Monk, Pauline Oliveros, and Laurie Anderson.

Expressionism: an early 20th-century movement that sought to reveal through art the irrational, subconscious reality and repressed primordial impulses postulated and analyzed in the writings of Freud. See Chapter 5: European and American Art Music since 1900.

Extended performance technique: non-traditional performance of an instrument (extended instrumental technique) or use of the voice (extended vocal technique) in order to extend its range and/or expand its timbre palette. This term is most often associated with American experimental music. It should be noted that a non-traditional performance technique in one culture may be a traditional performance method in another.

Folk song: a song of unknown authorship that has been transmitted through oral tradition and usually exists in various versions as a result of being passed on over time. Compare *art song*. See Chapter 6: American Vernacular Music.

Form: the structural aspect of music concerned with such factors as statement, repetition, contrast, and development of musical material. See Chapter 1: Elements of Sound and Music.

Front line: the members of a jazz ensemble whose principal function is melodic, in contrast to the harmonic, rhythmic role of the *rhythm section*. See Chapter 7: Jazz.

Fugue: title for a *polyphonic* musical work that is characterized by the development of a *theme* or *subject* through *imitation*. Most fugues are composed for four "voices," or independent lines in the texture, commonly identified by their relative ranges as soprano, alto, tenor, and bass. In the *exposition,* or opening section, the theme is presented by one of the voice parts alone and is then taken up by each of the other voice parts in turn. As each new voice enters, the others continue with counterpointing material and the texture becomes increasingly dense. In the entries—subsequent appearances of the theme in one or more voices—the theme may be stated in new key areas or altered form, for example, with durations of the pitches longer or shorter. Entries alternate with *episodes* in which fragments or motives from the theme are developed.

Gamelan: percussion *orchestra* of Bali, Java, and other Indonesian islands. See Chapter 2: Musical Instruments and Ensembles.

Gospel music: genre of American religious music. See Chapter 6: American Vernacular Music.

Harmony: the vertical dimension of multi-part music through which simultaneous combinations of tones produces *chords* and successions of chords. See Chapter 1: Elements of Sound and Music.

Heterophony: a variant of monophonic texture; adjective heterophonic. See Chapter 1: Elements of Sound and Music.

Homophony: a musical *texture* comprised of two elements, a dominating *melody* and supporting *accompaniment*; adjective homophonic. See Chapter 1: Elements of Sound and Music.

Imitation: the repetition, in close succession, of melodic and/or rhythmic material in one part by another part. See Chapter 1: Elements of Sound and Music.

Impressionism: an artistic movement of the late 19th and early 20th century pioneered by French painters whose muted colors, blurred outlines, and sensuous subjects influenced contemporary poets and musicians, most notably Claude Debussy.

Improvisation: extemporaneous creation of music. Many Western European composers were renowned improvisers (see for example biographies of Bach, Beethoven, and Chopin) and the ability to improvise is essential in such traditions as Indian classical music, African tribal music, and some styles of jazz, where the performers are the composers and the performance is the work. Improvisation often takes place within established conventions, involving preexisting material that the performer is expected to flesh out in the course of performance. Improvisations are sometimes recorded, or later written down based on memory. See Chapter 3: Composer, Performer, Audience and Chapter 7: Jazz.

Instruments/instrumental music: see Chapter 2: Musical Instruments and Ensembles.

Interval: the distance between two *pitches*. Often expressed as a number of *scale* steps or as the ratio of relative frequencies. See Chapter 1: Elements of Sound and Music.

Jazz: see Chapter 7: Jazz.

Key: *tonic* plus *scale* type, for example, G major, A minor. See Chapter 1: Elements of Sound and Music.

Mass: service in the Christian liturgy that culminates in Holy Communion, the re-creation of the Last Supper of Jesus and his disciples. Texts of the Mass have been set to music by composers from the Middle Ages through today.

Melisma: in vocal music, a single syllable of text sung on a lengthy succession of *pitches*.

Melody: succession of musical tones that is perceived as constituting a meaningful whole. See Chapter 1: Elements of Sound and Music.

Meter: organization of time in which *beats* are arranged into recurring groupings of two's, three's, or some combination of two's and three's. See Chapter 1: Elements of Sound and Music.

Mode: *scale* type, determined by the size and succession of *intervals*. Most music from the Western European tradition draws its pitch material from the major and minor modes.

Modulation: change of *key*. See Chapter 1: Elements of Sound and Music.

Motive: a short figure of distinctive melodic or rhythmic configuration that recurs throughout a composition or section and functions as a unifying element.

Monophony: single-line melody; adjective monophonic. See Chapter 1: Elements of Sound and Music.

Music theory: rules and principles of musical composition. Examples include rules of counterpoint associated with the Western European tradition, the principles governing the performance of raga and tala in Indian music, and practices of harmony and scales in jazz.

Musical theater: a play set to music for singers and instruments and performed on the stage with costumes and scenery. Dance is an important component of many musical theater works. Musical theater differs from *opera* in that dialogue is spoken rather than sung in *recitative*.

Opera: a large-scale dramatic production requiring solo singers, an *orchestra*, costumes, scenery, and often choruses and dancers. The word "opera," is the plural of "opus," the Latin for "work," suggesting the multidimensional nature of the form. China, Japan, Indonesia, and India are among the world cultures that have rich traditions combining music with other theatrical elements and performance arts for ceremonies and entertainment.

Oratorio: similar to *opera* except that the subject is religious and the stage performance is without acting, costumes, and scenery.

Orchestra: in its broadest sense, a large ensemble such as a symphony orchestra, marching band, and jazz band or orchestra. In addition to a size of about 12 to over 100 players, other features of orchestral ensembles are the division of the instruments into sections, direction of the ensemble by a conductor, and performance in comparatively large venues, such a concert halls or even outdoors. Counterparts to Western orchestral ensembles include the West Indian steel pan orchestra and the *gamelan* of Indonesia. See Chapter 2: Musical Instruments and Ensembles.

Orchestration: the part of the creative process that involves designating particular musical material to particular instruments.

Ostinato: from the Italian for obstinate or persistent, a clearly defined phrase or motive that is repeated persistently, usually at the same musical *pitch* and in the same musical part, throughout a section or passage.

Overture: a self-contained instrumental piece intended as an introduction to another work such as an *opera, oratorio,* or *musical theater*

Percussion instrument: see Chapter 2: Musical Instruments and Ensembles.

Performance artist: an artist that works in two or more disciplines at once, one of those disciplines being a performing art. An example would be a sculptor creating set pieces to include in a theatrical performance of their own creation.

Performance practice: the conventions and customs associated with the performance of a particular musical repertory—for example, the instruments employed, techniques of singing, and the nature and extent of improvisation that are expected. See Chapter 3: Composer, Performer, Audience.

Phrase: a fairly complete musical idea terminated by a *cadence*, which is comparable to a clause or sentence in prose. See Chapter 1: Elements of Sound and Music.

Pitch: the location of a musical sound in terms of high and low. See Chapter 1: Elements of Sound and Music.

Polyphony: from the Greek *"poly"* for many and *"phono"* for sound or voice, a musical *texture* comprised of two or more simultaneous melodies of fairly equal importance; adjective polyphonic. See Chapter 1: Elements of Sound and Music.

Polyrhythm: musical *texture* comprised of two or more simultaneous and independent rhythmic lines; adjective polyrhythmic. See Chapter 1: Elements of Sound and Music.

Prepared piano: the insertion of foreign objects (screws, bolts, erasers, plastic, etc.) between the strings of a piano to alter its timbre. See Appendix 1: John Cage.

Program music: instrumental music that portrays a story, scene, or other nonmusical subject. Composers generally identify the subject in the title of the work. Compare *absolute music*.

Raga: an ascending and descending pattern of melodic pitches used in music of the Indian subcontinent. See Chapter 8: World Music.

Ragtime: a genre of instrumental music from around the turn of the 20th century that is an important predecessor of jazz. Most rags are for piano and are based on a steady one-two, or oom-pah, *beat* in the left hand supporting a highly *syncopated* melody in the right hand. Scott Joplin was one of the most prolific composers of piano rags.

Recitative: a style of text setting, found especially in *operas* and *oratorios,* that closely follows the rhythm and accents of speech. Recitative is used primarily for narrative and dialogue and is characterized by *melody* of narrow range that follows the accents of the text, spare *accompaniment*, one *pitch* per syllable of text, little or no repetition of text.

Rhythm: the durational and temporal dimension of musical sounds. See Chapter 1: Elements of Sound and Music.

Rhythm section: in jazz, the instruments that keep the beat and provide harmonic support. Common members of the rhythm section are drum set, piano, string bass, and guitar.

Ritornello: from the Italian for return, the opening section of a work, particularly of *concertos* and *arias* of the Baroque period, that recurs either as a whole or in part between sections of contrasting material

Rondo: a musical form involving a principal *theme* that is stated at least three times in the same *key* and intervening subordinate themes in contrasting keys. The rondo was a favorite design of final movements during the classical period.

Rubato: a practice in performance involving changes in *tempo* for expressive purposes.

Sampler: a device that allows the user to digitally store, manipulate, and play back recorded sounds.

Scale: arrangement of the *pitch* material of a piece of music in order from low to high (and sometimes from high to low as well). Each element of a scale is called a "step" and the distance between steps is called an *interval*. See Chapter 1: Elements of Sound and Music.

Score: the composite of all parts of a notated composition arranged one underneath the others, each on a different *staff*. Conductors work from scores while performers read only their particular part.

Serialism: a compositional method in which the composer constructs a germinal cell, usually a series of pitches, which is then repeated over and over in various permutations throughout the course of a work.

Solo: from the Italian for alone, the term is used for the part in ensemble music that is performed by a single player (the soloist), such as the solo part in a concerto, and also as descriptive of music intended to be performed by one player. In the Western tradition, the largest solo literature is for keyboard instruments or for members of the guitar family, all of which can create a complete musical texture without the participation of other instruments. There is also a small solo repertory for unaccompanied violin, flute, and other instruments that usually perform as part of an ensemble.

Sonata: from the Italian "*sonare*" the verb "to sound," a common designation for instrumental works to be performed by one player, for example, piano sonata, or a small group of instrumentalists, for example, sonata for violin and piano.

Sonata form: a structural plan that evolved during the Classical period and has been used to the present day as the design of symphonic, chamber, and solo movements. A movement in sonata form consists of three sections: (1) exposition that presents two principal themes and key areas; (2) development in which thematic material from the exposition is manipulated, varied, and elaborated; (3) recapitulation that restates the themes of the exposition, but both in the home key. This basic plan can be expanded to include an introduction and a coda. See Chapter 1: Elements of Sound and Music

Staff: the Western European system of horizontal lines and intervening spaces that has been used for the notation of *pitch* since the Middle Ages.

String instrument: see Chapter 1: Musical Instruments and Ensembles.

Strophic: a musical form in vocal music in which all verses of text are sung to the same music.

Subject: a *theme* or melody that constitutes the basic material of a composition, especially a *fugue*.

Symphony: a title applied mainly to orchestral music from the Classical period to the present.

Syncopation: irregular or unexpected stresses in the rhythmic flow. See Chapter 1: Elements of Sound and Music.

Tala: in music of the Indian subcontinent, the sequence of beats that underlies continuous cycle of rhythmic improvisations executed by a percussion player. See Chapter 8: World Music.

Tempo: rate of speed in music, often indicated by Italian terms such as *Allegro* (fast), *Andante* (moderate, walking pace), and *Large* (slow).

Texture: the quality of a musical fabric with respect to the number and relationship of simultaneous musical events. See Chapter 1: Elements of Sound and Music.

Theme: musical material, often a melody, that functions as a principal idea for a musical work, comparable to the theme of an essay or speech. *Fugues* typically have one theme; works in *sonata form* typically have two. During the course of a work, the theme may recur in its entirety or broken up into shorter *motives,* and it may appear in its original form or with *variations* in one or more of its elements, such as rhythm, tempo, melodic design, orchestration, or key.

Tone color: the distinctive sound quality of a voice or instrument. See Chapter 1: Elements of Sound and Music.

Tonic: the starting pitch of a *scale*, also called keynote.

Tutti: from the Italian for all, the full ensemble. In a *concerto*, passages for the soloist alternate with sections for the tutti.

Variation: a broad concept encompassing a number of procedures that modify musical material. Ornamentation or decoration of a melody, repetition of a theme with different orchestration or at a different tempo, reharmonization of a theme, including modulation from major to minor or vice versa are common techniques.

Vibrato: wavering or fluctuation of pitch.

Virtuoso: in general, a person of extraordinary skill and knowledge. In music, a highly accomplished musician.

Voice/vocal music: see Chapter 2: Musical Instruments and Ensembles.

Word painting: in vocal music, musical representation of individual words and textual images, for example, the use of high pitches for words like sky, low pitches for words like deep, and ascending pitches for rise.

Woodwind instrument: see Chapter 2: Musical Instruments and Ensembles.